CRES   10/15

FABER & FABER

has published children's books since 1929. Some of our very first publications included *Old Possum's Book of Practical Cats* by T. S. Eliot, starring the now world-famous Macavity, and *The Iron Man* by Ted Hughes. Our catalogue at the time said that 'it is by reading such books that children learn the difference between the shoddy and the genuine'. We still believe in the power of reading to transform children's lives.

→→ FABER CLASSICS ←←

Moondial

Helen Cresswell

Illustrated by P. J. Lynch

ff

FABER & FABER

Moondial was first published in 1987

This edition first published in 2015
by Faber & Faber Limited
Bloomsbury House,
74–77 Great Russell Street,
London WC1B 3DA

Typeset by MRules
Printed by CPI Group (UK) Ltd, Croydon CR0 4YY

A CIP record for this book
is available from the British Library

ISBN 978-0-571-32290-9

FSC
www.fsc.org
MIX
Paper from
responsible sources
FSC® C101712

2 4 6 8 10 9 7 5 3 1

for Anna,

who was there from the beginning

Lux et Umbra vicissim, sed semper Amor

(Light and Shadow by turns, but always Love)

The grounds at Belton House

PROLOGUE

It is midnight in that most dark and secret place. If you should chance – and why should you? – to be walking there, you would be blindfolded by the night. You would hear the hooting of a lone owl from the church tower, the scuff of your own steps on the gravel. You would smell the ancient, musty scent of the yews that line the path, and the curious cold green odour of dew on grass. You put out a hand. It gropes to find the ungiving touch of stone. The shock of it brings an uprush of fear so strong that you can almost taste it.

At that moment your fifth sense is restored. A slow silver light yawns over the garden. Shapes make themselves, statues loom. Ahead, the glass of the orangery gleams like water. You notice the shadow the moon has made at your feet as you would never notice a mere daytime shadow.

You stand motionless, with all five senses sharp, alert as a fox.

But if by some chance you should possess another, a sixth sense, what then? First a tingle of the spine, a sudden chill, a shudder. You are standing at a crossroads, looking up at a statue. A huge stone man seems locked in struggle with another, smaller figure, that of a boy. But the presence you feel is all about you now, and with a lifting of the hairs at the nape of your neck you are certain, *certain* that you are being watched.

You turn slowly, half dreading what you might see. But the path before you is empty. Your gaze moves to the great, moonwashed face of the house itself. The windows are blank and shuttered, though that strange sixth sense is insisting on hints, whispers, secrets.

The scene fades and you realize that the moon is going back behind the clouds, and then you run. And as you run through the disappearing garden you feel that a mighty wind is blowing and voices are clamouring in that empty place.

2

What you also hear, and what you will remember ever afterwards with a shudder, even in the full light of day, is the lonely sobbing of a child.

ONE

Even before she came to Belton, Minty Cane had known that she was a witch, or something very like it. She had known since she was tiny, for instance, about the pocket of cold air on the landing of the back stairs. (Though she could not have known that a man had hanged himself there.) She knew, too, that she shared her bedroom. She had woken at night to see shadowy presences gliding across the floor. She had never spoken to them, merely watched, sensing that they were on some silent business of their own. At other times she had seen blurred faces hovering over her, and pale hands floating like blossoms in the dark. There had been invisible footsteps, breathings.

She did not talk about these things for the simple reason that they did not strike her as remarkable. Their appearance was as commonplace to her as that of the milkman. The only difference was that the milkman did not cause her spine to prickle. When she was younger she had once or twice mentioned a dark visitor to her mother, who had talked vaguely of car headlights casting strange shadows, and curtains blowing in the wind.

During the past year Minty had also occasionally heard her father's voice and that, she knew, *was* remarkable, because he was dead.

Now she and her mother were living in a different, smaller house, and her mother was working full time at the hospital. Minty came home from school and found the house empty. The weekends, once oases, were now deserts.

'And when it comes to the summer holidays, we shall have to do something about you,' her mother said.

'What?' demanded Minty. 'Post me off somewhere, like a parcel?'

'That's an idea,' said Kate. 'Registered, of course.'

'Wonder what it'd cost,' Minty said. 'What stamp you'd have to put on me? And where would you stick it? On my forehead?'

'I'm still trying to think where to post you *to*,' Kate said.

In the end it was decided that Minty should spend the holidays in the village of Belton, and stay with Kate's godmother, Mrs Bowyer.

'You'll like that,' Kate told her, and Minty agreed that she probably would.

Mrs Bowyer lived in an old stone cottage right opposite Belton House, which was golden and beautiful and had once belonged to Lord Brownlow. Now it was owned by the National Trust, and was open to visitors from April to October.

'I'll get in free, I expect,' said Minty, 'whenever I want to, with Aunt Mary working at the House, and that.'

Once Mrs Bowyer had been in the service of the Brownlows, like her mother before her. Now she helped out at the House sometimes, in the summer.

'What I'm dying to see,' said Minty, 'is that secret tunnel.'

'Not exactly secret,' Kate told her. 'Just hidden.'

'Same thing,' said Minty, knowing full well that it was not. 'And those little red frogs!'

'I'm not sure I believe in them,' said Kate. 'I never heard of such a thing! Frogs aren't red, in the first place.'

'Mud-coloured,' Minty said. 'Khaki.'

'And right next to the kitchens! Ugh!' Kate shuddered. 'I couldn't fancy to eat a thing!'

A tunnel ran from Belton House under a courtyard to the kitchens. According to Aunt Mary it was infested, at certain times of the year, with a plague of frogs. Only they were no ordinary frogs. They were red, a sort of dull, plant-pot red.

The night before Minty was due to go to Belton she thought she had changed her mind, and said so.

'I'd be all right here, Mum,' she said. 'And what about you? You'll be lonely.'

Sometimes her mother cried at night. Minty had heard her, sobbing softly and hopelessly. Left alone, she might cry every night, for six long weeks.

'I shan't have time,' said Kate firmly.' You'll enjoy it there, Minty.'

8

'What about Aunt Mary? I've never stopped with her before. Only gone to tea.'

'*I* stopped with her, when I was little.'

'Different thing,' Minty told her. 'What'll I *do* all day?'

'Well, you'll give Aunt Mary a hand, I hope, for a start. And then . . .' she paused. 'I don't know . . . I always thought of Belton as a . . . *happening* sort of place.'

'Happening?'

'Mmm. I don't quite know how to put it. But when I was little and stopped there, I had that front bedroom, you know, opposite the walls. And over the top of the wall I could see the roof of the orangery, and the church tower, and bits of the garden . . .'

'Well? What about it?'

'It's so long ago now . . . but I do remember having a feeling – it sounds daft, I know – a feeling that there was something happening . . . more to it all than met the eye.'

This, coming from Kate, was surprising.

'Ghosts, you mean? Haunted?'

'That kind of thing, but – well, more *real*, somehow. I don't know. I don't really remember. I never actually *saw* anything.'

'But I shall,' Minty told herself. 'If there is anything there, I shall know.'

'And, of course, I was only a child.'

'What do you mean *only* a child?' demanded Minty. 'I feel like a member of the human race to me!'

'You're not going for a million years, Minty,' her mother was saying, done with memories. 'And I shall pop out whenever I can, and see you.'

'Visit the prisoner, you mean?'

Minty was only saying this. She had changed her mind again about going to Belton. She had changed it the moment her mother had started talking about 'happenings'.

They drove there the day after school finished.

'What a pretty house!' Kate murmured as they drew up.

'Not bad,' agreed Minty. She liked the way the

garden was right on the edge of the countryside. Only a hedge divided the short grass from the long.

Aunt Mary was already at the front door as they went up the path. Minty dutifully kissed her cheek, powdery and faintly scented.

'If you haven't grown another three inches!' she exclaimed.

'Five centimetres,' Minty corrected. She had always been the tallest in her class, and when she was younger used to try holding her breath to stop herself growing. Whether this had actually worked she did not know, but she was now only the fifth tallest in the class, and not so touchy about it.

'Just in time for elevenses,' Aunt Mary said, and led the way to her sitting room, that smelled so strongly of the garden that it might have been part of it. It smelled of warm grass and roses.

Minty, happily scoffing scones, remembered what a good cook Aunt Mary was. After months of makeshift meals straight from a tin or the freezer, the food here would be something to look forward to. Half guiltily she checked the thought, which seemed disloyal to her mother. Kate had enjoyed cooking in the old days. Now she no longer had the time, and even when she had was often too tired. Nowadays, a really good meal was a treat, what Kate called a 'feast'.

'Come on, let's have a feast tonight,' she would say. 'What's on the menu? Roast guinea fowl ... peacock pie ... octopus soup ...'

Minty turned her attention to the others.

'She can always come across with me,' Aunt Mary was saying.

'Across where, Aunt Mary?'

'To the House,' Kate told her. 'Your aunt helps out in the shop some afternoons.'

'I like to be over there,' said Aunt Mary. 'Though it isn't the same as the old days, of course. All those people! Any Tom, Dick or Harry who can pay at the gate. Enough to make the Brownlows turn in their graves.'

'I've never quite understood how people *can* turn in their graves,' Minty remarked. 'Coffins aren't very wide. Or is it the whole coffin that turns? No, can't be. There's soil all round it.'

Aunt Mary looked startled, but was not to be deflected from her theme.

'Term times are the worst, of course,' she went on. 'Coachload upon coachload of children. You'd wonder where they all came from.'

Her eye rested on Minty, now into her fourth scone.

'Not that I've anything against children,' she said. 'Dear little things ...' she added vaguely and insincerely.

Minty choked.

'Not me,' she thought. She wondered if she were beginning to change her mind again about staying.

'I've put her in the same room as you used to have, Kate,' Aunt Mary said.

'Oh, she'll like that! Shall I take her up and get her unpacked?'

'You remember where it is? Door facing you at the top of the stairs.'

Halfway up her voice called after them.

'Do tell her to take care with the bedspread, Kate. It's my memory patchwork!'

Inside the room Kate went straight to the window.

'Oh – the view! Just as I remember it!'

Minty wondered why she should be so surprised.

'Views don't move,' she thought. 'Not fields, or houses, or churches. Especially churches.'

'Isn't it lovely!' Kate exclaimed. 'Don't you think so, Minty?'

'Yes, lovely,' agreed Minty, not really looking. It was *her* view, and she would look at it in her own time. Instead, her gaze went round the room.

There seemed to be a lot of pictures, for a bedroom. Most of them were paintings or photographs of Belton itself. This struck Minty as boring, considering that the real thing was straight across the road. There were some old brown photographs of ladies in starched uniforms, standing so stiffly to attention that they might have been starched themselves. These, she decided, must be of a younger Aunt Mary, and her mother before her.

14

She turned her attention to the bed, covered with the patchwork bedspread that she was to be so careful with.

'What's she mean, Memory Patchwork?' she asked.

'Oh, I remember her telling me about it ages ago,' Kate said. 'She's made it herself, with scraps of old dresses and curtains and things, from the old days. Her mother had saved most. People did, in those days. Never threw anything away. I daresay some of them are from the House – so it's full of memories for her, you see.'

'I expect so,' said Minty, who did not go in for memories much herself. 'I'll be very careful with it. I won't put muddy wellies on it or spill indelible ink or tear it to shreds!'

The two of them unpacked Minty's suitcase. They put her clothes in the lavender-scented drawers and wardrobe. The games went under the bed, the books and cassette player on the window-sill, and the old bear on the patchwork.

That's more like home!' said Kate, and it was.

She stayed for lunch, which was home-made steak and kidney pie, then raspberries from the garden.

'Nice to have someone to cook for,' said Aunt Mary.

'Oh, you'll find she's a good little eater,' Kate assured her. 'Not a bit fussy. Eat anything.'

'Except fried worms and deadly nightshade,' thought Minty, who was becoming tired of being discussed as if she were not there.

'I thought we'd go over and look at the church this afternoon before I go back,' Kate said. 'I don't believe I've ever seen it – not since I was a child, anyway. Are you still a church warden, Mary?'

She nodded.

'I've got the key, if it's not open. And the key from the graveyard into the garden. We keep things locked in the winter, of course.'

As Kate and Minty walked out of the gate they heard children's voices, screams and shouts, coming from their right. Minty brightened.

'That'll be the adventure place,' she said. 'It looks good. And that little train.'

On previous visits to Belton it had been closed.

'Lots of children there for you, as well,' Kate told her.

Minty said nothing. Grown-ups always thought that you could plonk any children you liked together and they would automatically get on. Nobody ever said, 'There'll be lots of grown-ups for you.'

There were only a few steps to take to the churchyard. The road was hot and empty, the village basking. It had the air of something that was waiting, breath held. They walked slowly up the path to the church, stopping to read tombstones. There was a strong churchyard smell of grass and stones and nettles, mingled with the hot dry scent of yew. Then Minty, going on a little ahead, had her first sign that she was stepping on the edge of a mystery.

A little icy gust blew about her. She was approaching the corner of the church. She stopped. Again she felt it passing over her face and bare arms. She shivered under the July sun. Looking up at the tower, she saw tiny gilt pennants, hardly bigger than leaves, glinting and quivering. In a wind they would spin, she thought, like weathercocks. But they did not spin. They stood motionless, while Minty stood and gazed, her skin brushed with ice.

She took a few testing steps forward and the coldness came with her. Another step, then another. All at once the air was warm again, and quiet. She frowned.

'Now this,' thought Minty Cane, 'is exceedingly strange.'

She turned and intently retraced her steps, and was instantly back in that inexplicable pocket of cold. She stopped again on the corner and felt the invisible wind (a visible wind would spin the golden leaves). She felt something else, too, with her sixth sense, and knew that the little icy whirlpool was only a message. The real mystery lay beyond.

'Listen to this one!' she heard her mother call, and did half listen to the old carved words on a tombstone, though she was really straining to hear other voices, other words.

Kate came up beside her.

'Minty?'

'Do you feel cold?' Minty asked.

'*Cold?* Today?'

'I mean just here. In this particular place.'

'Mmmmmm.' Kate did, indeed, suddenly wrap her arms about herself. 'In the shade, I suppose.'

'More than in the shade,' Minty thought, but said nothing. She would come again later, on her own, give those other voices a proper chance.

Then they were in the real dim and cool of the church itself, and Minty was reading all the plaques and tablets as she liked to do.

'Posh people,' she told Kate, not for the first time, 'are posh even when they're dead.'

This church was certainly exceptionally full of lords and ladies.

As they stepped out from the porch the heat struck them. Ahead, behind a high, wrought-iron gate, lay the gardens.

'Shall we?' Kate asked.

Minty shook her head, but hung back while her

20

mother went ahead. The air smelled centuries old and Minty suddenly had a curious feeling that time had stood still. So strong was this feeling of suspension that it was with relief that she saw Kate was still there, walking back towards the road. She, at any rate, had not stood still.

It came to Minty that if time *were* to stand still, a graveyard was the very place for it to happen.

'Because they're all dead,' she thought, her gaze travelling over the stones, crusted and lurching, oddly shipwrecked. 'And it makes no difference if you died yesterday or a hundred years ago. Dead is dead.'

She moved on deliberately and met the cold again. It was a deep, iron cold.

'Not my imagination,' she thought. She knew that she had a good imagination, because it said so on all her school reports. Herself, she was not even sure what it meant.

She stood licked by little icy tongues and tilted back her head again to see the top of the tower. The golden pennants were idle, stockstill.

'Or perhaps they *don't* spin in the wind,' she thought. 'Perhaps they're always like that, stuck.'

There was only one way to find out. She would have to wait until there was a real wind, an everyday wind that rocked the trees, billowed the washing on the line and blew smoke sideways, and then come and look. She could, of course, always ask Aunt Mary, but did not intend to. She had learned long ago to keep her secrets to herself.

Minty ran out of the strange cold and into the sunlight until she reached her mother. Kate put her arm around her and gave her a hug.

'Bless you,' she said. 'You'll be all right, won't you?'

'Of course,' Minty told her. She would have said this whether it were true or not. 'You're a goose.'

'I'll miss you,' Kate said. Minty, picturing her mother alone in their house when she went to bed, and alone when she woke up, knew that she would.

'Think how tidy the toothpaste tube'll be!' she said, and Kate laughed, as Minty intended her to. Sometimes Minty felt that she could work her mother as if she were a marionette, on strings. She wished she could feel that she would be able to manage Aunt Mary in the same way. They met her, just by the gate, coming from the opposite direction.

'I just popped over,' she explained. 'See how things are going. Selling lots of silly things, of course, to the children.'

'What sort of silly things?' inquired Minty.

'Oh, you know – little notebooks, and jigsaws and colouring things. Never mind – all the schools'll have closed by the end of the week, and we'll start getting proper visitors. Then we'll be able to move some of the quality stuff.'

'What sort of quality stuff?' asked Minty, innocently enough.

'We do have some very *nice* things in there, Minty,' Aunt Mary told her. 'Quality stuff. The National Trust doesn't go in for rubbish.'

'That was a lovely tea cosy you gave me at Christmas, Mary,' Kate said quickly. 'With that matching tea towel. Everyone admires it.'

23

As a matter of fact Kate had put both articles straight away into a drawer, saying they were too good forevery day. Loyally Minty kept her face straight.

'New line,' said Aunt Mary. 'It is pretty, isn't it?'

The three of them entered the house. There was a last cup of tea, and the goodbyes began. Minty and her mother went out alone to the car.

'You'd think it was forever,' said Kate, and gave Minty a final hug. 'Bye-bye, mumpkin. Be good.'

There was a break in her voice and Minty felt her own eyes water. Mumpkin! She hadn't heard that word for ages. It was part of a silly little rhyme that Kate had invented when Minty was only a baby.

'You're a madam and a mumpkin
And a pretty little pumpkin!'

'Time and again I'd say it, and oh, you loved it!' Kate had told her. 'And then, when you got older, you'd try to say it yourself, only you couldn't get your rs and ls right. "Pity pity pumpkin!" you'd say.'

Minty wanted to think the whole thing both embarrassing and daft, as it certainly was. The only thing was, that the lines really *did* start an echo in her own mind, they'd become part of her without her knowing it, all those years ago. They made her smile.

Kate got into the old orange car and started it up. Minty watched it turn, called a last goodbye, then stood till it disappeared round the bend. She glanced at her watch. Half past three.

It was just after four when the nightmare began. The time in between had already felt slow and strange. It was as if Aunt Mary's heavily ticking clocks were measuring a different, slower time than that in the world outside. Used to Kate's brisk movements, Minty thought that even Aunt Mary herself was moving in another, slower dimension. She moved like someone under water, or in a dream.

Minty went up to her room to listen to her tapes. Kate had bought her some headphones the previous day.

'I don't think your aunt'll want to hear *your* hundred best tunes from morning to night,' she'd said.

The room felt very hot, so Minty opened both the casement windows wide and leaned out for a breath of air. The sun struck a white blaze from the roof of the orangery beyond the wall. Minty's gaze moved to the left and the church tower, where those tiny gold pennants glinted, motionless.

'I know one place where I could get cool!' she thought.

But she would not go there again, not yet. Secrets, she knew, could not be forced. They unfurled, if you gave them time, slowly, like petals. You could not own them just for the asking. Either they gave themselves to you, or they didn't.

'After all,' she thought, 'if *I* have a secret, I don't have to tell anyone if I don't want to. Nobody in the world would know, unless I wanted them to. They wouldn't even guess I *had* a secret. And I have, already. I know about the cold wind blowing by the corner of the church.'

It was a shock to see Aunt Mary suddenly before her, lips moving but soundless. Hastily Minty pulled away the headphones.

'Sorry! Were you calling me? I couldn't hear, with these on.'

'Why not?' Aunt Mary sounded suspicious. 'I've been calling for ages. What are they?'

''Phones,' Minty told her. 'When I've got them on, I can hear the music, but nothing else.'

She wanted to giggle. Where in the world had the old lady been all her life, never to have heard of headphones?

'It's teatime,' Aunt Mary told her.

Minty followed her down.

'Headphones, stereo, computers, software,' she made a silent list of things that would be mysteries to Aunt Mary. 'Video, digital watches, calculators, microwaves ... she's living in a time warp.'

The table was set out properly for tea. It looked

as if every meal was to be a special occasion. Minty and her mother ate off their laps, or even standing, in the case of breakfast.

'That looks nice,' she said.

'I made you a jelly.'

They both sat down.

'Children like jellies,' remarked Aunt Mary.

'Here we go again!' thought Minty. 'Nobody ever says "Grown-ups like lamb chops"!'

'*I* do,' she said aloud. 'Especially orange.'

But that particular orange jelly would not reach her lips that day. Its unruffled surface would not be broken by the first spoon. The telephone rang.

'You get started,' Aunt Mary told her, and went into the hall to answer it.

Minty peered at the sandwiches. Some egg, some what looked like ham. She was on her second when Aunt Mary came back. Minty looked up at her, and that was the precise moment when the nightmare began.

Aunt Mary had changed. Her face was almost unrecognizable, very red, wild-eyed and almost

28

mad-looking. Minty, startled, stared, as if a stranger had materialized out of thin air.

Aunt Mary did not advance. She just stood there, staring back. A very long time seemed to pass with the pair of them frozen like a frame in a film. When they did speak, it was both at once.

'Minty, dear—'

'Is something the—?'

They both broke off. Politely Minty waited.

'Oh dear, oh dear!' Still Aunt Mary stood, and still she stared. 'Oh dear, oh dear, whatever shall I say? I've never in my life—'

Minty was alarmed. She had come to stay for five whole weeks, and it began to look as though Aunt Mary might be a little strange.

'Is something the matter, Aunt Mary?'

'Oh – oh yes, it is! Oh, it's terrible! I don't know how to—'

In the end, of course, she did. And when she did, Minty heard hardly anything after the first words.

'It's Kate! It's your mother! There – there's been an accident!'

What followed then Minty could hardly remember. It all seemed very slow and strange. An eternity passed, and then she actually heard her own voice screaming. It went out of her and froze in the air until it was followed by another scream, and another. As she stared, it seemed that Aunt Mary's head had swollen like a balloon, and was suspended crazily in air, red and monstrous.

Then Minty felt her whole body go into a violent shuddering, and now she seemed to be laughing. Hands came down heavily on to her shoulders and she was being shaken. She was being swallowed, and fought to escape. She tugged herself free, and a sharp blow on her cheek made her gasp with shock and pain. The palm of a hand struck her other cheek, and she drew a long, juddering breath, and was silent.

All at once it seemed her legs had gone to rubber, and she staggered a few silly steps sideways and fell on to the sofa. She closed her eyes because she wanted to go to sleep now and shut out the world. A numbness crept into her limbs. Even her brain was mercifully numb.

A long time seemed to pass before she felt herself terribly cold. She opened her eyes. Aunt Mary was sitting awkwardly on a dining chair. Her face was wooden. When her eyes met Minty's they were dull, unseeing almost. Neither spoke. It was as though they were in some terrible play, and both had forgotten their lines.

The truth was that the lines were there, but neither wanted to speak them. Minty did not want to ask what had happened to her mother, and Aunt Mary did not want to have to tell her. They both wanted to rush off the stage and into the wings, and hurry on out of the theatre, laughing with relief, and telling themselves that it was, after all, a play.

But it was not a play, and so in the end the words had to be spoken, and Minty heard that her mother's car had been struck by a lorry, and that she was at this very moment lying in intensive care in Grantham hospital.

'Can I go up to my room?' said Minty.

'You go on up, and I'll make us both a nice cup of hot sweet tea,' said Aunt Mary.

31

Minty did not take sugar, but could not be bothered to say so. She trudged up the stairs and into her room, where she dropped heavily on to the bed and the precious Memory Patchwork. Perhaps it did have special powers, as Aunt Mary seemed to think, because what came into Minty's head as she lay there was crowd upon crowd of memories. She thought of Kate at the seaside last year, paddling and splashing about with a huge net. She saw her ironing, washing her hair, hanging out washing, her mouth full of pegs. She saw her crying, laughing, frowning. Minty lay dry-eyed, watching a procession of pictures from the past because she did not dare conjure up a picture of the present.

Far away she heard the telephone ring. It seemed to come from another world. Then Aunt Mary came in with the tea.

'That was someone called John,' she said. 'Mr Benson. From your mother's office.'

Minty knew him. He came to the house sometimes. She liked him. He knew some good jokes and would play computer games, or help her with her maths.

'He's going along to the hospital now.'

Minty sat up.

'I want to go. Can I go?'

But Aunt Mary was already shaking her head.

'Not for the moment, he says. She's still having tests, and that. Head injuries, he said. Well, that's the main trouble, anyhow.'

'Why can he go and not me? She's my mother! I want to go, I want to!'

'Tomorrow, maybe. She'll be feeling better then, perhaps.'

Minty had seen pictures of people in intensive care. There were tubes everywhere. She had heard of people lying for weeks in a coma, while their family sat beside them and talked to them, hour after hour, in the hope of even a flicker of response. She did not believe that Kate would be feeling better in the morning.

'Better drink that and come along down,' Aunt Mary said. 'Better not mope up here on your own.'

Minty obeyed the suggestion. But a whole sunlit endless evening lay ahead. The sun was flooding in, making the house feel queerly dark and shadowed.

Aunt Mary turned on the television, but the screen was bleached and blurred. She drew a curtain across and the picture came into focus.

'Why not watch for an hour?' she said. 'Take your mind off things.'

She herself sat down and picked up her knitting.

'What can't be cured must be patiently endured,' she remarked vaguely.

'Could I go out?'

'Where? Where will you go?'

'I don't know. Anywhere.'

'There's nowhere much *to* go.' Aunt Mary sounded dubious.

'There's miles!' Minty thought of the fields and woods stretching out of sight.

'Oh, you mustn't go out of the village! Oh no, not on your own. You'll have to promise me that. I'm responsible for you.'

'If Mum was here she'd let me.'

This was true. 'I want you to go through the world fearless,' she'd say. Minty heard Kate's voice saying it now, and felt her eyes sting.

'I must do something!'

'Go over to the House, then. See if World is there, at the lodge. Nice, he is. Likes children.'

'World?' Minty echoed.

'Well, *Mr* World to you, I suppose.'

'Right!'

Minty went out. She had not the least idea what she would say to the nice Mr World who liked children, but it didn't seem to matter. She was leaving behind a table still laid for a tea that would never be eaten, and a telephone that might ring dangerously at any moment.

As she approached the entrance a coach swung out. It was filled with schoolchildren, homeward bound after their outing. Minty stared enviously after it. She could imagine how it was inside that safe cocoon, laps full of souvenirs and crisps, sweets being handed round, jokes told. Some of the children waved and she waved back mechanically.

She walked on. An old man was sitting in the doorway of one of the stone buildings to the left.

'Hullo, there!' he said. 'Not one been left behind, are you?'

'I live here,' she said. 'For the time being. With Aunt Mary, over the road.'

'Ah yes. Heard about you. So what's your name, then?'

She told him.

'That's a funny old name,' he said. 'Minty.'

'It's short for Araminta,' she told him with dignity. 'At least it's not two a penny!'

'Oh, it's not that. Can't say I've ever come across a Minty. It's an unusual name and, if I'm not mistaken, an unusual owner. Am I right?'

He was looking at her keenly, eyes bright in his all-weathers face.

'Come to meet the children, I daresay?'

'Children? Which?'

'Ah,' he said. 'That'll be for you to find out.'

'You mean there are children living in the House?'

How could there be? The House was open to the public, not a lived-in house at all.

'I never said anything about living.' His voice was low and he watched her closely.

'You mean ghosts?'

'I never said that, either. But the minute I clapped eyes on you, I knew. That's her, I thought! That's the one to turn the key!'

Minty shivered.

'What key?'

'To set 'em free! Those children! The ones I've known about sixty year and more. Only in snatches, mind. Only glimpses, and voices crying.'

'Crying,' said Minty softly, and felt an unbearable sadness welling up, a cold, orphan sadness.

'And they're locked up and crying and begging to be set free! I can hear their voices on the wind, and sense them in the shadows, and I fair ache sometimes, because they're there begging me, and I haven't got the key. But now you've come.'

'Yes,' said Minty. 'I've come.'

She hardly knew what the old man had been

saying, his words were only hints, clues. But she knew for certain that she had been given an invitation. It was an invitation into dark and perhaps dangerous places. But it was not one that she could refuse.

Two

Minty's night was wide and strange. She had lain for a long time before sleep came, because the Memory Patchwork seemed to be working its spell again. Memories were the only way to conjure up her mother now. She heard Aunt Mary's tread on the stair, and her own door opening. She shut her eyes and made her breathing slow and deep. She had never managed to fox her parents like this, but she foxed Aunt Mary now. She heard a deep sigh, and a whispered 'Poor child!' and the door closed again. There were footsteps along the landing, then another door opened and closed.

'Will there be any footsteps?' Minty wondered. 'Any figures at the end of the bed?'

She did not think so. She would have known already. She got out of bed and went to the window. She could make out the tower of the church, the faint watery gleam of the orangery and beyond that the shape of the House itself. Could there be children imprisoned there, as World said? Were they there now, chained in time and darkness, crying to be set free?

'I haven't got the key,' he'd said. 'But now you've come.'

As she leaned over the sill a strong night smell of green came up from the garden, and with it a rush of excitement, a sense of being on the threshold of a great adventure.

'I am Araminta Cane and I have the key! I am Araminta Cane and I have the key!'

She found herself whispering the words aloud, and the mere saying of them seemed to make them a certainty. And it seemed that they were being witnessed by invisible listeners who swarmed out there in the summer dark. And having spoken the words she felt more peaceful and went back to bed.

'Goodnight, Mother Goose!' she whispered, and fell asleep.

But the night was long with memories and

dreams. She could hardly tell where one ended and the other began, they made a tapestry. When she woke next morning she felt that she had been strangely comforted.

She lay and looked about her and thought of Kate, all those years ago, a child herself, lying and looking at those same walls and pictures. Now she was lying in a white hospital bed, and with this thought Minty felt the dread return.

She got up and went to the bathroom. It was most perfectly spick and span, with candlewick mats and little painted jars and bottles. On the stool was a basket filled with scented soaps, from which Minty had been told to pick her own. She had chosen honeysuckle. Now, as she washed, she thought of going through the day ahead smelling of honeysuckle, and wondered if it would have made all the difference if she had chosen wild rose, or lavender.

'This will be a honeysuckle day,' she told herself as she dressed, and even smiled at the thought.

She heard the telephone ring, then the murmur

of Aunt Mary's voice. She found that she was cold and that her fingers were trembling so that she could hardly fasten her buttons. Down she went into this strange new world with its unfamiliar sights and sounds and smells.

'Ah, there you are, dear!' Aunt Mary was determinedly bright. 'Did you sleep well?'

'Yes, thanks. Was that the hospital on the phone?'

'Oh, you heard it, did you? I was going to have left talking about it till after breakfast. Shall I fry you some bacon and egg?'

'I don't really think I want any breakfast,' Minty said. 'What did they say?'

'Well . . .' Aunt Mary was clearly going to pick her words carefully. 'She's still in intensive care. Still unconscious. But . . . but – comfortable.'

Minty did not see how you could be comfortable or uncomfortable if you were unconscious.

'Can I go and see her?'

'Well, yes, they say you can, but—'

'When? Now? This morning?'

'This afternoon. That Mr Benson will fetch us

in his car. Now come along and sit down and have something to eat.'

Aunt Mary did not want to talk about it. She probably did not even want to think about it. She wanted her mind to be as tidy and cosy as her house.

'But it's better when you do talk about things,' Minty thought. 'When Dad died, Mum said we were to talk about it all we wanted. And we did, too, and sometimes it made us cry. But somehow it got less and less bad.'

'Are you sure I can't fry you some bacon?' Aunt Mary was saying. 'And egg?'

Minty shook her head and fought back a wave of sickness.

'I'll just have cornflakes, please.'

She did not want even those, but to force them down would be easier than arguing. After breakfast, she announced, she would go over and explore the House and gardens.

'World said I could go over whenever I wanted.'

'I told you he liked children,' said Aunt Mary.

But when Minty passed his lodge the door was closed.

'House doesn't open till later,' she realized.

As she walked she liked the feel of the morning, still cool and dew-smelling and the air somehow uninterrupted and brand-new. She turned left and could see the silvery blue slates of the house gleaming, and the entry to a courtyard beyond.

'I could be walking into the past,' she thought.

The courtyard was deserted, but she could smell bacon, and hear the news being read on the radio. She looked about her, hesitating. She noticed a clock with a blue face on the coachhouse roof.

'Showing the wrong time,' she thought, without surprise.

Her gaze travelled right to the furthest corner. There was a door, slightly ajar. Minty approached. Cautiously she pushed it open. There was another door beyond, also open. She passed between the cold stone-smelling walls and gave that a push, too.

'The garden!'

It lay quiet and faultless under the early sun.

There were lawns, straight paths, yews and statues. Minty stepped on to the terrace and felt a thrill of recognition. She had never been here before, she knew, and yet had a strange knowledge that she was now stepping exactly where she was *meant* to step. This garden had been waiting for her.

Slowly she walked along the terrace. She paused to look up at the statues, as if expecting a sign on their stone faces. But they gave none. They gazed as they had always gazed, untouchable, intact. One was carrying stone fruit and flowers, the next was a lady with a flightless bird – a dove, perhaps. Now she went down the seven wide steps to the path that led to the centre of the garden.

No sooner had she done so than she became aware of being watched. She turned. No one was there. She lifted her eyes to the house itself. The windows were blank. She walked on, alert now, expectant. She had a curious sense of being drawn, of having no choice. As she went she was taking steps that had already been measured for her. She lifted her eyes and saw ahead, at the crossroads of the garden, another statue, and felt a prickling of her shoulderblades. There was a power in the air, so strong that she could hardly breathe.

Minty stopped in front of the statue, with icy tides washing her from head to foot. There were an old man and a young boy, both winged like angels, though she was certain that they were not. They seemed to be wrestling, struggling for possession of a bowl above their heads and, catching a glimpse of a metal beak, Minty suddenly realized what it was.

'A sundial!' she exclaimed softly, and then, almost immediately and without knowing why – 'Moondial!'

And as she spoke the word a cold distinct wind rushed past her and the whole garden stirred and her ears were filled with a thousand urgent voices. She stood swaying. She put her hands over her ears and shut her eyes tight.

The whispers faded, the wind died. Minty opened her eyes and was blinded for a moment by the sun. But when she did see, she knew that she was

in a now-altered morning, not at all the morning she had woken up to.

Slowly she wheeled about. It seemed to her that under the changed sky the very garden had shrunk. She lifted her eyes to the house itself and saw smoke rising.

'There was none,' thought Minty. 'Not when I last looked!' and started to run back the way she had come.

She had reached the little stone passage that led to the courtyard when she met the boy – bumped into him, almost.

'Oh!' she gasped. 'Sorry!'

The boy, too, jumped back. He stood staring at her so pop-eyed, jaw dropped, that she almost laughed.

'Oh my aunt! Oh my!' He was backing away, eyes enormous in his thin white face.

'What's the matter? Are you all right?' Minty said, while part of her mind had already taken in his dress, the rough jacket and queer woollen trousers, and knew that what she was seeing was what most people called a ghost.

'Oh ... oh!' he quavered. 'I ain't never seen one that *talked* before!'

'Who *are* you?' demanded Minty, affronted by this remark even though she did not understand it.

'I'll shut my eyes,' he said to himself. 'Then, when I open 'em – she'll have gone!'

'What cheek!' said Minty. '*I* will, then!'

She did so, though she did not in the least wish the boy to vanish. When she opened her eyes again it was just in time to see him cautiously unscrewing his own. They stared for a moment, then burst out laughing.

'Don't look as if we are going to disappear,' he said. 'Neither one of us.'

'No,' agreed Minty.

'Seen ghosts before, you know,' he continued. 'Well, bits and bobs of things, anyhow. But in broad daylight – and plain as the nose on your face!'

'Nor me,' said Minty. 'Here – what do you mean, ghost? *You*'re the ghost!'

He laughed.

'Oh *yes*,' he said. 'I'm a ghost all right. That's why

Cook told me to just run out for some raspberries for the pie. Run here, run there – wish I *was* a blessed ghost, and that's a fact!'

'I,' Minty told him coldly, 'have just come over from my Aunt Mary's house, and I don't think I imagined that!'

'Look,' he said, 'you could've just hopped out a rabbit-hole, for all I care.' He surveyed her narrowly. 'You're a bit of a let-down, for a ghost. I must be out of my head standing here rattling to you. I'd best be off and fetch them raspberries, if I don't want a whacking.'

'No! Wait! I've got an idea!'

'What?' His pinched white face was all at once alert, suspicious.

'Let's – let's shake hands!'

'Why?'

'Don't you see? Whichever of us is a ghost won't be able to, not properly. Ghosts go through things, they're not solid.'

He put out his hand and stared down at it, and shook his head dubiously.

'Don't like the idea of it. Ugh! My hand going straight through yours! Ugh! Fair makes you shudder!'

'It won't,' Minty told him. 'It'll be the other way round. If *I* dare do it, why can't you?'

He looked at her.

'You're a girl, aren't you?' he said. 'Dressed in boy's clothes.'

She nodded.

'Blessed if I'll be beat by a girl,' he said. 'Here, then!'

He thrust out his hand, his face screwed in a grimace as if expecting to touch something cold and slimy, and Minty put out hers. Their hands met and clasped. Warm solid flesh met warm solid flesh. The pair of them stood, hands locked, looking into one another's face in wonder.

'We're both real!' said Minty softly at last. Then, 'What's your name?'

'Tom,' he said. 'Short for Edward.'

She laughed delightedly.

'I'm Minty. Short for Penelope.'

51

They were still holding hands.

'You a downstairs too, then?' he asked. 'What are you? Laundry? Scullery?'

'What are you?' she countered.

He shrugged. His face clouded and he pulled away his hand.

'All sorts. They've not decided. I'm up from the London house. Footman's what I'm after.'

'Footman?'

'I ain't big yet,' he said, 'but I shall be. Country air. Keep taking big snuffs of it, and I'll be six foot before Pinch knows!'

He took a big, sniffing breath, as if expecting to add half an inch to his height then and there. Instead, he fell into a bout of coughing. He bent double. His coughs were dry and racked.

'I suppose it must work the other way round,' Minty observed. 'I used to hold my breath to stop myself growing.'

Tom short for Edward straightened, gasping for breath.

'*Stop* yourself?' he said. 'Whatever—? Oh. You're

a girl. Forgot. You'd never be a footman if you grew to seven foot, let alone six.'

'How old are you?' asked Minty.

He shrugged.

'Twelve abouts, I s'pose.'

'Don't you know?'

He shrugged again.

'Near enough, I do.'

'You've only got to ask your *mother*,' Minty told him.

'Dead.'

'Oh!' She was aghast. I'm sorry! I didn't—'

'And my pa.'

Minty stared. Suddenly she wanted to run away. She was looking at an orphan, and the very word orphan was terrible to her. It was a word that had been hovering perilously on the darkest edges of her own thoughts, a word she had tried to beat off as if it were a great black bat.

'An orphan,' he said.

Now the word was out, too late for her to clap her hands over her ears.

'Got brothers and sisters, though.'

Here was a straw, and Minty clutched it.

'Oh, that's good!' she cried with an enthusiasm that sounded ridiculous even to her own ears. 'I wish I had!' – this, at least, was genuine.

'Not that it matters a deal,' he went on, 'seeing I never see 'em!'

Calamity after calamity.

'Oh – but why not?'

'I'm here, see,' he told her patiently. 'They're there – in London. Two of 'em's dead, anyhow.'

Minty stared at him. She simply could not take in all this death so casually spelt out. In her world, grandparents sometimes died, or perhaps a neighbour, hardly known so never missed. She was the only person of her age she knew whose father had died. She remembered how this had marked her out at the time. People had seemed to tiptoe round her, leaving a careful space between them and her. She had seemed to stand alone in an invisible circle.

This boy stood in acres of loneliness.

'Don't you miss them?' It was all she could think of to say.

'Bit.' Then, after a pause. 'Miss our Dorrie, a bit. Funny nugget, she is. Makes me laugh.'

'How old is she?'

'Seven or eight abouts. Tried to keep her with me, I did, but they said she was too little. Would've liked her with me.'

His thin white face pulled long and sad. Minty could think of nothing to say.

'Still 'n all, once I'm six foot and a footman I'll have her here, all right!'

He took in several snuffing breaths as if to hurry this moment forward but he ended by coughing again, dreadfully.

'Needs some antibiotics,' thought Minty, wisely, and was about to say as much when a shout came from behind her.

'Here – you –whatsyername – boy!'

Tom straightened, eyes still watering, and Minty turned. A man stood there, leather-aproned and gartered, a gardener, she guessed.

55

'You coming for them raspberries or ain't yer? Birds've had hours at 'em already!'

'I'm – I'm coming now, sir!'

'You come here. Come on.'

Tom went and Minty watched. The boy looked skinnier and smaller than ever standing before the great burly man.

'New from London, ain't you?'

Tom nodded.

'Yes, sir.'

It was as if he were trying to make himself smaller now.

'Ain't heard of dawn, in London, I daresay. Or birds.'

Tom was silent.

Then the big man began to speak in a voice surprisingly soft and to punctuate his words with swift cuffs on Tom's head.

'*Birds* get up at *dawn*, whatsyername. Birds go peck, peck, peck –' (three swift cuffs, using both hands) – 'and they go—'

'Oh, don't!' cried Minty, but she might never have

spoken for all the notice he took. 'It's my fault he's late – he was talking to me!'

'*Boys* from *London*,' went on the terrible gardener, 'wants *learning* what's *what*!'

Tom had his hands up to his head now, to protect himself.

Minty ran to him.

'Stop it!' she cried. 'Please!'

But the soft voice and the cuffs went on, she might as well not have existed.

'*Stop* it!' she screamed and with her fists started to pummel the man and—

'Oh!' She gasped to find herself standing and aiming punches at the empty air. 'Oh!'

She let her hands fall, and as she did so had a swift, unmistakable memory of the feel of leather. She spread out her hands and looked at them, and they too seemed to be sending a message to say that they had, if only for a fraction of a second, beaten like birds against that vanished man, and could still remember the feel of that cold leather.

Slowly Minty looked about her and saw that the

57

morning had changed again. Before she even lifted her eyes she knew that the smoke would no longer be rising from the chimneys.

What happened . . .? she wondered. What did I do to make time jump? For that matter, what did I do in the first place to go back all those years? A hundred, at least . . .

Her gaze moved towards the centre of the garden and she remembered. Sundial . . . moondial . . .

Slowly she retraced her steps, following the way she had taken earlier – how many minutes, hours, centuries earlier? She came to the seven wide steps and the stone lady with the stone bird. She took a deep breath and slowly descended.

'I'll see if I can make it happen again,' she thought. She pushed away the ragged, half-formed thoughts that were warnings of the riskiness, the downright danger of what she was doing. If she succeeded in going back to that particular moment how could she be sure that this time she might not have to stay there, trapped forever, lost?

She drove the thoughts away by concentrating

very hard on the path ahead. She noticed that it was lined on either side by dark yews alternating with lighter evergreens, cut round like Christmas puddings. Between these were small stone plinths and urns with carvings of fruit and flowers.

As she drew near the sundial the prickling began between her shoulderblades. She thought, It will happen again.

She was wrong. She reached the sundial, and again she thought ... sundial – moondial ... but there was no rushing wind. There were no voices. She stared up at the boy wrestling with the man, and it was as if she, too, were wrestling, with time itself. She gritted her teeth and *willed* the wind and the voices, but they did not come. She felt only the strong sense of being on the edge of mystery. The mystery itself eluded her.

'Damn!' she cried at last, and stamped her foot.

And with that, even the sense of mystery departed. She was left high and dry in the present moment, alone.

'All right!' she said out loud. 'But I *will* get back – you'll see!'

And she went back the way she had come, out of the garden, out of the grounds and into the cold, inescapable present.

After a desert of time Minty was sitting in the back of Mr Benson's car and on her way to see her mother. A drive out was evidently a treat for Aunt Mary. She kept up a bright chatter, pointing out this and that. She remarked on the abundance of roses this year and on the lushness of the uncut verges. Perhaps she was simply avoiding the issue in the only way she knew, Minty thought. She was bright with a terrible determination.

Mr Benson said little. Minty was aware from time to time of his eyes glancing at her reflection in the driving mirror.

'I think,' he said carefully, in one of the rare pauses, 'that I ought to warn you, Minty, before we get there. What to expect.'

'You mean about the tubes and things? I've seen it, on television.'

'All those dreadful gory medical programmes,' put in Aunt Mary.

'I expect you have,' he said. 'But you still have to be prepared. All those monitors and screens, and the tubes too, of course.'

'I think I do know,' said Minty, but her voice sounded thin and scared even to herself.

'And – you won't find it easy to see Kate – to see your mother – as ... it's difficult to explain. You see ... she's not *there*, in a way ...'

'Just asleep,' supplied Aunt Mary.

'No. Not just asleep. Much further away than that ...'

He means almost as if she were dead, Minty thought. Because you can't wake her up. She saw vague images of the Sleeping Beauty ... Snow White ... That was how her mother would be. In the kind of sleep that cannot be broken by a shrill alarm or a shake of the shoulder ... only by a kind of spell.

'But – you mustn't be frightened,' Mr Benson was saying. 'She is still there.'

'Of course she is,' said Aunt Mary. 'It's

marvellous what they can do, these days. I've seen it on the television.'

'And not only that,' he went on, 'she will probably know that you are there, somewhere, deep down.'

Minty leaned forward, suddenly eager, but Aunt Mary was already saying, 'Oh, I'm sure that can't be true! Not if she's in a coma . . .'

Minty's eyes met those of Mr Benson in the driving mirror. She tried to make her own say, 'Thanks for trying!' and nodded her head for good measure. A flicker of a smile showed that he had received and understood her message. After that they left Aunt Mary to her roses and verges.

As the swing doors opened Minty met the warm, dry, antiseptic and unmistakable smell of hospital.

'It's only a smell,' she told herself, 'and Mum says she likes it!'

She was very determined to be brave.

'Fear isn't a real feeling,' Kate had told her, more than once. 'It's an instinct, and doesn't mean very much, really. Lots of things are bigger than fear, and can beat it. Love, for a start.'

As her legs went clockwork-wise along the polished corridors between the gleaming walls, Minty silently repeated the words as a kind of charm.

'Love for a start, love for a start, love for a start . . .'

Also, as a kind of counterpoint, she prayed, 'Let her eyes be open and see me, let her eyes be open and see me!'

But Kate's eyes were not open. They were closed, in a pale, remote face. Her head was swathed in bandages. All the tubes and wires that Minty had imagined were there, in a room where machines sighed and breathed, and green lights flickered on screens. A tiny bleep, irreverently like that of a computer game, monitored heartbeats that were certainly not visible under the stiff white sheets.

Minty stared. What was happening, she decided, could not possibly be happening. It was a nightmare, or a play. She was herself improbably draped in purest white, and wearing a cap and gauze mask. She was dazed by the unreality of it all.

The lights are very bright, she thought, and felt a tear slide down her cheek.

'You're only pretending,' she silently told her deaf and blind mother. 'You'll shoot up at any moment, and say boo!'

'Boo!'

Aghast, she heard her own voice. It echoed in that vast clinical quiet. Then a nurse was beside her. Minty looked at her – or rather at her eyes, which were the only human part visible.

'It doesn't matter if you talk to her,' said the invisible mouth. 'In fact, it's good if you do.'

Minty thought she detected a smile behind the mask.

'But nothing too sudden.'

A pause.

'What's your name?'

'Minty.'

'Oh. How – pretty. Unusual. Don't be frightened, Minty. Talk to her if you want.'

'Her name's Kate,' Minty heard herself say. 'Not "her".'

'Of course.'

Minty looked back at her mother, and could hardly forgive her. She had gone away into a peaceful darkness and left Minty stranded in the glaring light among strangers. The enormity of the betrayal was too much to take in.

'I think I want to go now,' she said, and turned.

'Oh please – don't! I know it all looks terrible, with—'

'It's not that.'

'Just say hello. Just say a few words.'

Minty turned back.

'Hello, Kate . . . Mum . . .'

She could not. What was she supposed to say? That she had had chicken pie for dinner and Aunt Mary says how good the roses are this year? Or dangerous, dark feelings that had no words, and even if they had could not be spoken in the presence of a stranger? Her eyes met those of the nurse.

'It's no good! I can't!'

She fled then. Down the gleaming corridors she sped, escaping from nothing into nothing. How she found herself outside the hospital again she hardly knew.

'D'you think it would have helped if I'd gone along with her?' she heard Aunt Mary say. Then the reply.

'I half expected it. Think of the shock. It'll be better next time.'

They all got into the car.

'I don't want to say a single word all the way back,' Minty heard her own voice say. 'Don't talk to me.'

Then, after a pause, 'Please.'

The car went between the amazing roses and knee-deep verges but Minty's eyes were as blind as Kate's. There was a murmur of voices from the front seat, but she did not hear what they were saying. She was in a kind of no man's land.

'I feel like a ghost,' she found herself thinking, and remembered the strange meeting in the garden that morning, and was oddly comforted.

She seemed to see again the altered sky and feel the touch of leather just before it had melted at her fingertips. It was all more real to her than what was happening now.

'I'll find him again,' she thought. 'I must!'

'I think I'd like to look at the House this afternoon,' Minty said. She had worked out that if Tom was anywhere, then it must be there.

'That *is* a good idea,' Aunt Mary said. 'Take your mind off things. Educational, too. You come along with me, when I go over to the shop.'

They went over by what Aunt Mary called 'the back way' – through the churchyard, past the orangery and the pool and into the stable yard.

It was hot again, and windless. As Minty followed her aunt along the path by the church an ice-cold breeze brushed her.

'Still there!' She paused, and tilted back her head. The gilt pennants glittered motionless. Aunt Mary trotted on ahead, oblivious.

'*She* never felt anything,' Minty realized, and ran to catch up.

'Off you go then, dear,' said Aunt Mary when they reached the stable yard. 'Got the guidebook?'

Minty nodded.

'Just tell them who you are. You'll be all right.'

Minty walked round to the front of the House and climbed the stone steps. Two large cast-iron dogs guarded the doorway. She stepped into the great hall, the floor chequered black and white like a chessboard. Minty advanced cautiously. Whenever she and Kate visited places like this she always felt as if she were in church. She felt that you should walk on tiptoe and speak in whispers.

She passed through the high, hushed rooms with their elaborate furniture and rich drapes, and knew that Tom could not possibly be here.

She stared up at the rows of gilt-framed portraits. Several were of children, plump and dressed in velvets and silks, like little kings and queens.

'He's not one of them!' she thought.

'D'you like them?'

She turned. An elderly man with a guide's badge was smiling at her.

'If you'd been a girl in those days you certainly wouldn't have been wearing *those*!'

He gestured towards Minty's jeans and sneakers.

'I don't know how happy children were in those days,' he said. 'They never quite look like children to me. More like miniature adults.'

'Mmm. I know what you mean,' Minty agreed.

'And in this particular family . . . I don't know . . . My grandfather used to talk about them when I was small. And you know what he used to say?'

'What?'

'There's one missing.'

'One – what?'

'Child.'

Minty gave a swift, involuntary shiver.

'No one ever knew what he meant by it. But his memory certainly went back a long way. "There's one missing . . ."'

He shook his head.

'So there you are!'

'Is the House ... are there any ghosts?' asked Minty.

'Oh, there's some story about the Queen's Bedroom,' he told her. 'Star-crossed lovers.'

'That's not Tom!' The words were out before she knew it. The guide seemed not to have heard.

'Seen the underground passage, have you? To the kitchens?'

'The kitchens! Of course!' That was where Tom would be – he had come to the garden to fetch raspberries for the cook.

'Which way are they?'

He directed her through a labyrinth of rooms and passages, and she found herself in a dim stone corridor with steps leading down.

'Now!' she thought. Her heart beat hard and fast. Might she really meet him again?

Then an outer door opened and there was an inrush of light and of excited voices.

'Don't push, children!'

Minty turned and sped back the way she had come.

'That's put paid to that!' she thought.

She reached the room with the portraits.

'That was quick!'

'Too crowded,' she told him. 'I'll go another time.'

She decided to save upstairs for a rainy day. Glancing through the window, she saw that she was looking straight down the yew-lined path that led to the sundial. And she knew, even as she felt her skin break out in goose-pimples—

'Out there somewhere, in the garden . . .'

She longed to rush out to it, then and there. But the garden was full of daytime visitors and anchored fair and square in the twentieth century.

'Later!' she whispered the promise. 'Later . . .'

It was evening before Minty came to the garden again. As she passed, World was there in his doorway.

'Well now,' he said, and looked at her hard. That's a white little face. It's your mother, isn't it? I've been hearing. Right sorry I am.'

She nodded.

'You keep going to where those children are. You need them now, I reckon, as much as they need you.'

That was all. She nodded again and carried on, as if taking an evening stroll into another time were the most natural thing in the world. She crossed the gold-flooded courtyard to the doors that led to the garden.

'You mustn't try to see him,' she told herself. 'The more you try, the harder it will be. Just feel. Just let things happen.'

Though as she set foot on the wide terrace she did allow herself to whisper:

'It's me, Tom short for Edward! I'm here!'

She gazed down over the lawns and paths with their steepling shadows and saw that they were quite deserted.

'Tom!' she whispered again. Tom!'

Silence, except for the clear whistling of birds. Slowly she moved past the tall statues with their locked-in secrets and down the seven shallow steps.

'No one in the world,' she found herself thinking. 'No one in the whole wide world.'

She moved like a sleepwalker, blindly, because her eyes were filled with tears. She went straight ahead as if pulled by invisible strings towards the sundial at the crossroads. And she reached it without seeing it until the last moment, and as she brushed her eyes and looked up at it, there again were the wind and the voices.

'Sundial – moondial!'

Her mouth filled with rushing air and she felt her hair fly out and she threw up her arms to steady herself as the ground seemed to rock under her. She felt as if she were drowning in a whirlpool.

Then the wind dropped, the voices faded. Minty opened her eyes. Shut them. Opened them again.

Dark! The garden was swallowed into night! Minty shivered. The blackness was total. Was it night?

'Can't be?' she thought.

But she smelled the icy tang of dew on drenched grass. An owl called. Then the moon came from behind a cloud and she saw the garden making itself again under her eyes in patterns of black and silver.

She wheeled to see the bleached face of the house and pallid wreaths of smoke rising into the stormy sky. It was not only night, it was a night centuries old.

'Now what ...?' she wondered. She dared not stir so much as a foot away from the moondial because she knew that it was her only anchor – her anchor in time.

And so she waited for something to happen, because she knew that something must, else she would not have been brought here. And as she stood, the centuries-old night – she could not tell how many centuries – began to feel comfortable to her. She settled into it, as if time itself were settling about her. She was at ease.

Then came what she had been waiting for, and when it came, it was not what she had expected at all.

Faintly, far away, she heard a child's voice, singing. She stood stockstill. The hairs at the nape of her neck stirred.

The singing came from the direction of the house, and Minty strained her eyes for a glimpse of the singer.

> *'Poor Mary sits a-weeping, a-weeping,*
> *a-weeping,*
> *Poor Mary sits a-weeping on a bright*
> *summer's day . . .'*

The voice was high and flutey. It wove through the darkened air with a dreamlike wandering that seemed to show that it was singing to itself.

> *'Oh what is she a-weeping for, a-weeping*
> *for, a-weeping for,*
> *Oh what is she a-weeping for on this bright*
> *summer's day?'*

The voice floated into the empty summer night of the invisible child singing out of the darkness.

> *'She's weeping for a playmate, a playmate,*
> *a playmate,*
> *She's weeping for a playmate on this bright*
> *summer's day . . .'*

And then the moon went behind a cloud again.

THREE

The silence was so long, the dark so deep, that Minty thought that now she must be altogether out of time – time and place. Then, closer now, came the child's voice again.

> *'Girls and boys come out to play*
> *The moon doth shine as bright as day . . .'*

Minty drew a deep breath, then herself joined in the song, though her voice was wavering.

> *'Leave your supper and leave your*
> *treats . . .'*

The other voice broke off suddenly, leaving Minty to finish the song alone.

The moon gleamed behind ragged clouds. Standing quite close was a small, cloaked figure.

'Who is it?' The voice was hardly a whisper. 'Who's there?'

'Don't be scared – it's me!'

As Minty spoke the moon shone full, and all at once the figure had a shadow. She had a glimpse of a small pale face and then, with a snatching movement, a hand caught up a hood and pulled it over the head.

'She's very small,' Minty thought. 'Younger than me – must be!'

The hooded figure edged a little closer.

'Are you from the village?'

Minty nodded.

'Yes. I'm Araminta Cane.'

She hardly knew why she used her full name – she rarely did so.

'Do you . . . know who I am?'

'No. Please tell me.'

'You . . . haven't heard . . . what they say . . .?'

Minty shook her head.

'No. But listen . . .'

She wanted to tell this child that she was a visitor not just from the village, but from another time. Forgetting the danger, she stepped eagerly forward, but the child shrank back and pulled the hood across her face.

'What's the matter? Don't be frightened! I'm not a ghost, I'm—'

'Sarah! Sarah!'

A shrill voice rang over the quiet garden and with it the spell was shattered. The little figure hesitated. Minty had a glimpse of huge, scared eyes, and then the child turned and hurried away, back towards the house.

'There you are, little devil!'

'Please, please! I'm sorry, I'm sorry!' sobbed the child as she ran, frantically pulling up her skirts as she stumbled in her haste.

'There!' came the woman's harsh voice. 'See what you've done! You've frightened the moon away!'

And as she spoke the moon did, indeed, go

into hiding. The distant cloaked figure, tiny now, dissolved into the dark.

With the new dark began a new journey in time. Minty stood perfectly still as she felt the shift, the wheeling of day and night, seasons and weathers. Eyes closed, she yet sensed the light and shadow by turn, felt heat and cold, wind and rain. She smelled violets, roses, damp leaves, and even thought she felt the sting of snow on her lips.

She heard wind roar, voices whispering, children singing, and then, suddenly close and real, a voice she knew:

'Dandelion – what's the hour o' the day?'

Time had stopped again. Minty let out a long, shuddering sigh. She did not need to open her eyes to know that she was still a visitor, not yet home.

'Ah!' said the voice. 'That fetched you, right enough! Knew it would. Phooo! Four o'clock!'

Minty opened her eyes to see Tom short for Edward sprawled nearby and blowing the last feathery seeds from a dandelion clock.

'Four o'clock!' he repeated.

'It certainly is not,' she told him. 'It's seven, at least. And don't think you brought me here by blowing *that*!'

She gestured scornfully at the bare dandelion stalk.

'How else, then? Thought of you, didn't I, while I blowed!'

She looked at him and saw how thin and pale he was, and remembered the gardener's relentless buffeting of that morning, and did not have the heart to argue.

'All right,' she agreed. 'You brought me here.'

He grinned and jumped to his feet.

'Not the first time I've tried, neither,' he admitted. 'Days I've tried to get you back!'

'What d'you mean?' She was amazed. 'It was only this morning we met!'

'Oh lummee! Oh gracious! Oh *hark*!'

'It was!'

'Days back,' he informed her. 'I should know. I'm the one that lives here. You ain't. You ain't neither scullery nor house nor anything else, so don't you go telling any more of your tales, Miss Minty short for Penelope!'

'No, I'm not, of course I'm not! And why should I pretend? After all, I'm from the present. You're from the past.'

He surveyed her thoughtfully.

'Don't know what you're talking about,' he said at length. 'Present?'

'Now,' she told him, irritated by his confidence, and irritated, for that matter, by his really thinking he had summoned her merely by blowing a dandelion clock.

'Now?' he echoed. 'What's now?'

Before she had time to think up a suitable reply he answered his own question.

'This –' he spread out his arms about him, ' – is now. This very minute. Look – see that?'

She followed his pointing finger and saw a butterfly, a pale blue one she had never seen before, just alighting on a stone.

'Yes,' she said.

'There, then! So it's now, ain't it? Now for you, and now for me!'

She considered the matter. There seemed no denying it. Her gaze went beyond him to the house. Smoke rose from the chimneys.

'His now,' she thought. 'His time.'

Then she realized that even the time of day was different, let alone the century. She had entered a garden of evening cool and shadows. Now she felt the heat of the sun on her bare face and arms.

'But it's only now for you,' he continued, having evidently himself been working things out, ''cos you're a ghost!'

'Don't say that!' Minty gave him a swift slap.

'Ouch!'

'There! Not a ghost! Go on – say it!'

'Well – maybe not to me. But old Maggs never saw you, the other day.'

'The gardener, you mean?'

He nodded.

'Gave me a proper walloping,' he said ruefully.

'I saw him. Horrible man. But listen – I touched him – I could feel his leather jerkin. I felt it, and then—'

She broke off. She had felt the cold leather, and

almost in the instant it had melted into thin air.

'Then what?'

'He vanished,' she admitted slowly. 'And you.'

'There you are, then!' He was triumphant again. 'But he didn't vanish for me – and don't I wish he had!'

Minty pondered.

'Why did you want to see me again?' she asked. 'Why did you blow that dandelion?'

He shrugged.

'Someone to talk to, I s'pose. Told you – Dorrie and the others stopped in London.'

His face was all at once downcast, troubled.

'Have you heard any news – about Dorrie?'

'Bit. Coachman give me a message. Stopping with old Mother Barker. Know what *that* means.'

He grimaced.

'What?'

'Bits of crusts, that's what – and that's if she's lucky. And night and day – gutter-picking! And she's only little! Here – grown any taller, have I, since last week?'

'This morning, you mean,' thought Minty, but wisely said nothing.

'Not really ...' she told him. 'Not so you'd notice ...'

He stood drawing in huge gulps of air but ended, as before, half doubled up, coughing violently. When at last he straightened up, Minty said:

'I think you might've grown a *bit*, now I look at you ...'

She lied because she, too, found it unbearable that his little sister should be half-starved and gutter-picking. She willed him to grow tall and strong and wear a footman's livery, so that he could send for Dorrie, fill her with bread and butter, and make her laugh.

'*I* reckon I have.' He was standing so straight he was almost on tiptoe. 'Here!' He lowered his heels. 'Why are you dressed like that, if you're a girl? What's your job?'

'I – I haven't exactly got one,' she said. 'I'm on holiday.'

'Holiday? What d'you mean?'

'From school.'

'You . . . school? You mean – reading and writing!'

'Well, yes. But I learned them ages ago.'

He was gazing at her, shaking his head.

'Where did I get you from?' he asked himself. 'Still – least you don't go running off, like the other one.'

'What – other one?'

'Oh, you ain't my *only* ghost, don't you think it!' he told her.

'Who's the other, then?' She felt jealous, almost.

He frowned a little.

'More . . . more a *real* ghost than you . . .' he said. 'Always at night when I see her . . . littler than you, and dressed like a proper girl, with long skirts.'

Minty stared. Could they both share a ghost, from yet another, earlier, time?

'What's she look like?' she asked. 'What's her name?'

'Never seen her face, not proper,' he admitted. 'Got this long cloak, and a big hood. Seems

86

scared when she sees me, as if *I* was the ghost!'

He laughed at the very idea.

'Know what her name is, though.'

Minty waited, knowing what he would say.

'Sarah!'

'Oh my moon and stars!' She shivered in the heat.

Time, it seemed, was a web, and all three caught in it – herself, Tom, Sarah . . .

'What's up?'

She looked straight at him, daring him to disbelieve.

'I've seen her, too. Just now. Just before . . . I came here.'

'What? In broad daylight – plain as I see you?'

'No. It was night, like you said. But not my night. *Her* night.'

He was gaping now.

'Oh, *I* don't know!'

'You *don't*!' he told her.

'Nor you! You don't, either!'

There came a distant bellow.

'Here – you!'

Tom whirled about and his eyes stretched in fear.

'It's him! Maggs!'

He took to his heels. No goodbye, not even a wave. Minty hesitated but only for a moment.

'Wait – wait – I'm coming, too!'

'Suit yourself!' The words floated back to her.

'I will!' she thought.

As she reached the top of the seven steps he was already disappearing.

'Wait!' she called, but he had gone.

Again she hesitated briefly. Then she ran on. It seemed to her now that she had nothing to lose, that one reality was as good as another. In the narrow entry she ran almost straight into him, just as on their first meeting. He was standing pressed against the wall of the passage, flat as a shadow, anxiously scanning the courtyard beyond.

'Tom!' she whispered.

He turned.

'Got to wait till the coast's clear!' he whispered back. 'Ain't let in the garden, unless I'm sent. Only went to see you. I won't half catch it if *she* finds out.'

'She? Who?'

'Mrs Crump!'

She peered past him into the courtyard beyond and knew now that beyond a shadow of doubt she was in another century. Before, she had only the silent witness of smoke rising from the chimneys.

There was a coach, emblazoned with gold and the now familiar insignia of the Brownlow greyhounds. The courtyard was crammed and crisscrossed – grooms led steaming horses, footmen strutted, porters unloaded boxes and trunks.

'Look!' Tom hissed. 'That's James – First Footman! Oh lardy and look – his legs are slipping!'

Following his finger, Minty saw the footman parading. His long face wore a practised, curling sneer. She saw, too, strange bulges in his stockings, just below his calves.

'Don't he think he's it!' Tom whispered delightedly. 'Poor old peacock – tried to pad his calves, and got himself legs like lumpy porridge!'

Minty laughed with him, jolted out of her awe by this certain sign that these were real people she saw. A figment of the imagination would never have slipping calves.

'Best make a dash for it!' Tom scanned swiftly about. 'You coming?'

She nodded.

'They'll not see you – not a daylight ghost. Still, here, take this! And don't run – walk!'

He snatched up an empty pail and thrust it at her, then set off, hands in pockets, into the courtyard. Minty, clutching the pail, followed, wincing as it creaked and clanged.

'Help!' A thought struck her. '*I* may be invisible – but what about the bucket?'

She dropped it with a tremendous clatter. It went rolling on its side over the cobbles. It seemed to roll for an hour.

'Hey – boy!'

She stiffened.

'Pick it *up*!'

She stared at the speaker, a gap-toothed man in gaiters, then started after the bucket.

'Leave it!'

Tom swiftly turned back, righted the pail, and touched an imaginary cap.

'Sorry, sir!'

'You get off back down where you belong!'

'Yes, sir, sorry, sir!'

Tom scurried down the side of the yard and disappeared into a doorway.

'In for a penny in for a pound!' thought Minty, and followed.

Safely indoors, on home ground, Tom slowed his pace, then turned.

'Still there, then!' He shook his head disbelievingly. 'Can't somehow seem to take it in. You not vanishing, I mean, like the others.'

'You're sure it *is* only you who sees me?' Minty asked. 'You don't think they saw me out there?'

'Dunno. Didn't dare risk it, though. That's why I fetched that bucket – to stop 'em going for you.'

'Oh! I thought you picked it up for the same reason I dropped it.'

'You dropped it? On purpose?'

'Don't you see? If I *am* invisible, even then the

bucket might not've been. What if they'd just seen a bucket floating along in mid air!'

'Oh lummee!'

He laughed, he bent double with mirth, and ended up coughing and laughing together.

'A – ghost bucket!' he spluttered. 'Oh *lawks*!'

He leaned against the wall and surveyed her.

'Tell you what,' he said. 'Let's find out.'

'Find out what?'

'If they can see you. You come along of me, now, to the kitchen.'

Minty's heart began to thud again. Before, she had been in the open. If she ran fast enough, she could escape. Now she would be entering an unknown warren of stairs and passages. She would have to cross that underground tunnel with its mysterious red frogs.

'I dare you!'

'Right!' she said.

'You're spunky, I'll say that,' he told her. 'Remind me of our Dorrie, a bit. Oh my – what if old ma Crump does see you, and throw a fit! Crump the

Grump – hope she *does* throw a fit and foams at the mouth and her eyes drop out!'

'Very nice,' said Minty. 'And what about me?'

'Come on!' he said.

She followed him through a labyrinth of stone-flagged passages, turning flights of stairs. She wished she had a ball of twine to unravel behind her, a lifeline if she had to escape.

'Or a piece of chalk to make arrows,' she thought. 'Or even a few biscuits to crumble, like Hansel and Gretel.'

Their footsteps echoed – or was it only Tom's, she wondered?

All at once the tunnel she had heard of stretched before them. It was higher and wider than she had imagined, and dimly lit by oil lamps, hung from the roof and walls. The air was chill, faintly musty, smelling of damp brick and stone. It settled like winter on her warm arms and face. To enter the foreign cold of this flickering tunnel seemed the *real* step backwards in time.

But Tom was already ahead, with shadows

that rocked and spoked about him, a long-legged spider.

She followed. Fear made her blank, shuttered her eyes and ears. She did not even remember the plague of frogs. Afterwards, she dimly recollected that on her left had run a kind of railway line, with trucks and wagons.

Now, however, the air began all at once to smell warm and yeasty. She sniffed eagerly the comfortable scent of new-baked bread. It was a sign of everyday, it helped to anchor her.

They were almost at the end of the tunnel. Tom turned.

'I gotter try to get in without *her* seeing,' he said.

Minty nodded. 'So have *I*!' she thought.

''Ere!' She heard a voice from the kitchen shriek. 'You let go that dripping pan, you thieving miss!'

Tom stiffened, then slid round the door, that stood ajar. Minty drew a deep breath and followed.

She blinked in the sudden daylight and shrank from the clamour about her. She had not known a kitchen could be so crowded.

'*You* know whose that dripping is!'

The speaker was a red-faced woman whose head was encircled by a white frilled cap tied under her chin, like some monstrous baby. She banged the stolen bowl on to the table with one hand and fetched the culprit a box on the ears with the other.

'Please, Mrs Crump, I was only—' the girl whimpered.

'Don't you give me any of your onlys, miss,' retorted Mrs Crump. 'You get on and scour them pots, you hear, else I'll scour *you*!'

The kitchen was full of people who seemed to be scouring pots, or filling them, or banging them. Minty saw that Tom had himself seized hold of a broom as proof, she supposed, of his industry.

'Nobody's noticed me,' she thought. 'I *must* be invisible!'

Nonetheless she felt uncomfortable because people seemed to be nearly seeing her, looking just past her ear, perhaps, or even straight at – and presumably, through – her. Tom caught her eye and winked, but she frowned.

'Here – you – boy!'

Mrs Crump moved remarkably fast for so stout a personage. She wove deftly through her minions and had Tom by the ear.

'Ooowch!'

Minty let out a cry in sympathy, and was reassured to find that she was apparently inaudible as well as invisible.

'You – whatsyername – what was that wink?'

'Please, ma'am, nothing, ma'am, I—'

'Wink, wink, wink!' With each word Mrs Crump gave a severe tweak to Tom's ear, as if trying to turn a particularly stiff tap. His face changed from its usual pallor to a crimson as furious as her own.

'I ain't *having* winking in my kitchen, d'you hear?'

Another mighty twist.

'At this rate,' Minty thought, 'he soon won't hear anything – not out of that ear, anyhow!'

'You ain't *here* to wink, whatsyername, you ain't paid fifteen shilling a year to wink. You come alonger me, and I'll put you where you can wink yourself blind!'

She sailed straight towards the door, still with Tom by the ear. Minty had to jump out of her way. She did not feel like finding out whether they would go straight through her. She did not feel that she could bear it. To be invisible was one thing, to be mere thin air was quite another.

Minty hurried down the tunnel after them.

'There!'

Mrs Crump flung open a door and pushed poor Tom inside.

'You stop there and wink, whatsyername, and get all them bottles dusted and tidied, while you're about it!'

She slammed the door. She rummaged in an enormous bunch of iron keys that hung at her waist.

'There!' she cried triumphantly as the lock clicked.

She turned so abruptly that Minty was caught offguard and to avoid being walked through jumped into the open doorway of the next room. Mrs Crump stopped. She stared in. Minty held her breath. Had she become all at once visible?

'And I'll have that one locked, as well!' she decided.

Next minute the door was slammed and the key turned in the lock. Minty was aghast. She seized the handle of the door and rattled it.

'Let me out! Let me out!' she screamed. She listened for a reply, or returning footsteps. Silence.

'Tom! Tom!'

There was no answer, so she ran and beat her fists on the wall that divided their prisons. But she sensed the absolute, ungiving denseness of the stone, and her arms fell.

'I'm trapped,' she thought. 'Double trapped – in time, and in here!'

She looked about her. She was evidently in the Victorian equivalent of the cupboard under the stairs. Brooms leaned against the walls in rows. There were brushes with long handles, brushes with short handles, brushes for blacking, scouring, cleaning bottles. Buckets stood in neat ranks as if drawn up for inspection. Then there were large stone pots of some candlelike substance,

honeycomb-coloured. Minty leaned over and sniffed.

'Beeswax!'

Could she eat it, she wondered, if she remained a prisoner for days? She would rather not.

The room was intensely quiet, with the stillness of a tomb. And it was the silence that unnerved her.

'I'm alone!' she thought, and slid to the cold floor, leaning her back against a cupboard.

And then loneliness took hold of her, the loneliness she had been pushing away, keeping at arm's length. It came in cold, slow waves and she sat hunched, head bowed on her knees as it washed over her. She was enveloped in a kind of blackness that was the feeling of fear, almost indistinguishable, as if loneliness and fear were the same thing.

And mixed in with it came voices, pictures.

'Dead . . . an orphan . . .'

A picture of her mother carved in marble on a high white bed.

A high, solitary voice:

100

'*Poor Mary sits a-weeping, a-weeping,*
  a-weeping,
Poor Mary sits a-weeping on a bright
  summer's day . . .'

Minty found herself weeping. The warm tears
trickled on her fingers.

'Oh Mum, Mum!' she sobbed. Then, 'I'll talk to
you next time, I will!'

And as she wept the loneliness dissolved and,
with it, time. She went again through the dark and
the whispering voices, floated weightless till she
came to rest quite effortlessly, like a bird alighting.

In the sudden different silence she heard birds
singing a song of sunlight and felt the warmth of sun
on her head and arms.

'I'm back!' she whispered. She opened her eyes
and saw that she was in the garden again. She
welcomed the present moment now, almost stroked
the warm grass in her thankfulness.

She got to her feet and slowly approached the
stone sundial ... moondial. Even now she felt its

pull, its power. She gazed at the two winged figures, the man and the boy.

Who were they? Bearing the sundial ... moondial ... as seasons turned, years wheeled, centuries rolled? Their stone limbs were pitted by time and weather and yet they seemed immutable, could stand till Doomsday ...

Minty put out a hand and half fearfully touched the stone hand of the winged boy.

'I'm on *your* side!' she found herself whispering, and even as she spoke felt the air change and thicken, heard faint voices of children singing ...

She snatched her hand away.

'No!' she cried. 'No!'

And she ran away, hands over her ears, through the deserted garden.

Next day Minty went to the hospital alone.

'There's no point in my going,' Aunt Mary said, 'when she doesn't even know I'm there. Give her my love, though,' she added.

Mr Benson called for Minty soon after breakfast.

'We don't need to worry about visiting hours,' he said. 'You can visit any time you like. Feeling better today?'

'Yes, thanks,' she said, and it was true. She was not sure exactly why, but felt that it was something to do with yesterday's adventures in the garden. If she could reach Tom and Sarah, who were lost in time itself, then she could reach Kate. However far away she seemed, she was at least in the here and now.

When she stood in the brightly lit room where Kate lay, nothing had changed. The machines still sighed and breathed, the busy green lights flickered.

'Hello, Minty,' the nurse said.

'Hello.'

Minty advanced to the bedside and looked down at her mother.

'Mum, it's me, Minty,' she said. 'Don't go away, please!'

'Why don't you sit down?' the nurse said, and indicated a chair. Minty drew it up and sat. She gazed again in silence. She had meant to talk to Kate, but what could she say? She looked up and saw that the nurse was watching her.

'Listening, too,' Minty thought. 'She'll listen to every word I say.'

She leaned forward and spoke very softly.

'Mum, Aunt Mary sends her love.'

No sign showed on that perfectly white face.

'And so do I,' she added lamely.

Several minutes passed.

'Where *is* she?' Minty wondered desperately. Then, 'What can I *say* to her?'

What would she say if Kate were with her properly, her usual self?

'Would I tell her about Tom and the moondial?'

She knew that she would not. It was a secret. She longed to share it, but knew that it was too fragile, too private. Kate was the one person in the world who would believe her, but even she would say, 'Oh Minty – I've never known an imagination like it!' or joke, 'Why don't you bring Tom home for tea?'

In the very moment that Minty realized this, she had the idea. It was so sudden and perfect that she actually felt her heart jolt.

She leaned forward, forgetful of the nurse.

'Listen, Mum, I've had an idea. All kinds of funny things have been happening to me at Belton. You'd never believe them if I told you. But I've got to tell someone, I've got to! Listen, Mum, and I'll tell you what I'm going to do ...'

She glanced up and met the curious eyes of the nurse. It was no use. She lowered her voice to a whisper, leaned so far over that she felt Kate's light breath on her cheek.

'I'm going to tell you a story, and it's the story of what's happening to me. I don't even know what the end will be.'

She paused.

'It's lucky you're like this,' she told the unconscious Kate, 'else I wouldn't be telling you at all. First instalment tomorrow.'

She rose, then bent and kissed her mother's forehead.

'As if *I* was the mother,' she thought, 'and her the child.'

She looked at the nurse.

'Is the doctor here? Could I ask him something, please?'

'Oh! I think so. If you go to the desk and ask – I have to stay here.'

'Thank you. Goodbye.' She paused. 'Goodbye, Mum. Don't forget what I said!'

The doctor had a young face with old lines and Minty liked him at sight. He listened to her properly, she could tell that.

'Absolutely!' he said when she had finished. 'Marvellous idea! And – what about some music to play between instalments? Got any favourites, has she?'

'You've got to swear,' Minty said, 'that you will never, ever listen. Do you?'

'I swear. Cross my heart and hope to die.'

'And you've got to make the nurses swear, as well. Especially *that* one.'

She paused.

'If you don't, I shan't do it.'

'I'll make them. If they don't, I shall kick them out.'

She smiled.

'Sounds like a very special story you've got to tell,' he said.

'Oh, it is. The kind of story you never tell, usually.'

'But these are very special circumstances. That it?'

She nodded.

'Then your mother's a very lucky lady. And she'll hear that story, Minty, never you fear. She's a long way away at the moment, resting somewhere, but she's there. And the one voice in the world she wants to hear is yours.'

Without warning tears rushed to Minty's eyes. She nodded dumbly.

She turned and went and he called after her:

'But you'll come yourself sometimes, won't you?'

'I will!' she called back.

Mr Benson drove Minty home to fetch the Walkman and tapes.

'I was going to suggest it myself,' he said. 'About the music, anyway. It's amazing how it works. Music often gets through where nothing else will.'

'Except my voice,' said Minty jealously.

'Of course. That's taken as read. Going to tell her a story in instalments, are you? That should keep her hanging on there.'

'Not just any old story, either,' Minty said.

'I love your mother too, Minty,' Mr Benson said after a pause.

'Everyone does,' said Minty flatly. She did not want to listen to him. He said no more.

When she entered her house Minty felt as if she had been away for a hundred years. Everything seemed dead, lifeless, foreign. And surely it was never as silent as this? The bowl of fruit, the jars on the kitchen sill, looked like a still life. The furniture stood stiff and awkward. The very air was thinned and desolate.

'Perhaps rooms don't come alive till people live in them,' Minty thought.

She found what she wanted as quickly as possible

and felt relief when she stepped outside again into the warm, live street.

'Look, Minty,' Mr Benson said as they drove the few miles to Belton, 'you won't want to be going to the hospital every day, now you've got the tapes. But when you do want to go, just give me a ring, and I'll fetch you. Right?'

'Right. Thanks.'

Minty found Aunt Mary in the garden, deadheading roses.

'The more you pick them, the more they come,' she remarked complacently. 'Well, dear, how did you find your mother today?'

'Is that true?' Minty sidestepped the question. 'About the roses?'

She liked the idea of the dead flowers everlastingly renewing themselves, tumbling pellmell out of the tall stems. It seemed a kind of magic.

'Oh yes,' Aunt Mary said. 'You wait and see.'

She looked particularly pleased with herself – excited, almost, as if she expected new roses to unfurl like party streamers under her fingers. It turned out that the explanation was quite different.

'I've had ever such an exciting morning,' she told Minty. 'I've had a visitor!'

'Oh. Who?' Minty asked, not caring.

'Ever such an interesting person. A Miss Raven.'

The name struck a chill. Minty shivered involuntarily.

'Doing some research, she says, for a book she's writing. About ghosts, of all things!'

'Ghosts?' Minty had a sense of danger, threat. Could it be that others knew about the children, besides herself and World?

'And – are there any?' she asked.

'Oh, as to that,' Aunt Mary said, 'I don't believe so myself for a single moment. If there were, I'm sure I should've seen them myself, long before now.'

Minty doubted this. She doubted whether Aunt Mary would see even a hooded phantom deadheading roses right by her elbow. Not even if it had blood dripping from its fingers.

'But *some* say so. You know how these tales spring

110

up around old places. There are stories about the Queen's Bedroom. And some tale about a giant footman who worked here years ago.'

'Nothing about children,' Minty thought with relief.

'Anyway, she wants to stop for a while, while she investigates, she says. And bless me, I haven't told you the most exciting news of all!'

'Oh? What?'

'She's going to stop here, with us. We're going to have a lodger!'

Minty shivered again.

'Someone walking over my grave,' she thought. And then, 'Or theirs.'

Four

Minty went back to the garden that afternoon with a strong sense of foreboding. As she entered the drive up to the house she saw the bent figure of World moving slowly back to his post. She watched him treading the hummocky grass.

When he had greeted her she put her question.

'Has there been a woman here, asking things?'

'There's lots of women come here asking things. You'll be meaning the one who calls herself Raven.'

Minty nodded.

'I told her nothing,' World said. 'She was a woman I wouldn't tell the time of day. Not with the cold eyes of her, and the thin lips. I told her nothing.'

'But she's coming to stop – she's stopping with my Aunt Mary!'

'It'll be the children she's after,' World said. 'And it'll be for you to save them.'

'But how – how can I?'

World shook his head.

'I would, if I knew the way. It's as I told you. There's only you has the key. Found 'em yet, have you?'

'Yes. Well, one of them, and perhaps two. But I still don't really know—'

She broke off. Some deep, sure instinct told her that she must not speak about the moondial. It was gathering a strong power into itself, she felt it already. But it was a power that had no words.

'I'll save them,' she said. 'I will!'

She left him and went through the courtyard and into the gardens, but knew that she was wasting her time. There were visitors wandering up and down the straight paths, even standing by the moondial itself, all unaware of its power.

Nonetheless she walked towards it, and as she drew near felt its pull again – even now, surrounded by other people, strangers. She stood looking up at it and addressed it silently. Then a thought came to her so clearly that it was as if a voice spoke.

'What happens to time, when the moon shines on a sundial?'

With the question came a cold, distinct draught of air. She had been posed a riddle.

'Thank you,' she whispered, and accepted it.

And she walked on while her mind reeled with the enormity of the question. Moondial – measuring a different time. Moondial – free from the slow, relentless march of the sun, the trickle of sand in the glass, the minute by minute ticking of clocks. Moondial – freewheeling, measuring the real time of hearts and lives and linking them across centuries.

Moontime!

She had been walking without realizing it towards the far end of the garden and now, coming to herself, saw ahead the iron gate that led into the churchyard. Still dazed, she walked through it, and found herself at the foot of the tower. Gooseflesh rose on her bare arms.

'Of course!'

She had quite forgotten. It was still there, that mysterious, icy pocket.

'I know!' a voice said.

She turned, and without surprise saw Tom standing there.

'Brrr!' He, too, shivered. 'Just as if someone'd walked over me grave!'

He looked about him.

'Don't look much different,' he said. 'Except it's daytime, of course.'

Minty did not understand.

'I'm not sure how I did it this time,' she admitted. 'And I didn't *feel* anything, like I did before.'

'What d'you mean, "did it"?' he said.

'Got into your time.'

He grinned.

'Ah, but you didn't, Miss Clever! Thought you was the only one knew about the moondial, didn't you?'

She was blank.

'*My* turn to be invisible!'

'You mean—?'

'Queer, though, ain't it, getting here? Like going through a sort of tunnel, and a big strong wind blowing.'

She looked beyond him, through the gateway and into the garden. The afternoon visitors wandered there, stalked by their sharp shadows under the unmistakably twentieth-century sun.

'Believe me?'

She nodded. Then she remembered.

'Tom – listen! I've got to warn you! There's someone after you!'

He laughed.

'They won't come looking here, not Maggs or Crump or nobody! All fast asleep, they are. Hey – and that's a rum thing!'

He had his head tilted back and was looking at the top of the tower with its tiny gleaming pennants.

'An owl hooting up there, not a minute ago! An owl! Where's *that* gone flapping off to?'

Minty laughed despite herself. He was happier than she had ever seen him – carefree, as if he were on holiday. In a way, he was, she supposed. It seemed a shame to spoil it. But the menacing Miss Raven was on their track, and he must be warned. She tried again.

'No, Tom, listen! It's not Mrs Crump I mean, or Maggs – it's a woman from my time. She's—'

'Hey! Look! Look at *that*!' He let out a soft whistle. 'Ladies – with *legs*!'

A group of women was wandering up the path towards them, guidebooks in hand.

'Where's their skirts? Oh my! Wait till I tell our Dorrie this!'

He started to caper towards them.

'Watch this!' he called. 'My turn to be invisible!'

Minty watched, horrorstruck. It was even more impossible that he should be invisible than it had seemed for herself to be. Surely they could see him?

But he was dancing about them now, making mock bows, pointing at their bare legs. Now he was thumbing his nose, waggling his fingers on his ears, pulling outrageous faces.

'It's so peaceful here!' sighed one of the party.

Minty giggled. She clapped a hand to her mouth.

'Hello, dear,' one of the women said.

Behind her, Tom grimaced fiendishly.

'H-hello. I'm – I'm just laughing at a joke I thought of!' She felt that some explanation was necessary.

'Ah, what it is to be young!' the woman said.

'Ain't it *just*!' said Tom – and vanished.

'Oh!' Minty cried.

The group moved past her and went into the church. Minty waited, then whispered:

'Tom! Tom!'

Silence.

'Come on back!' she hissed.

But he had gone. She felt his absence as clearly as if it were a presence. He had spun back through that whirlpool of wind and voices and was back in his own time.

'In the dark,' she thought. 'All on his own. Poor Tom!'

She was still standing in the icy patch by the tower. She noticed a tiny headstone, a mere thumbnail of a stone. It said, quite simply: E.L. 1871. It was probably that of a child, she thought. But if so, why did it not say that it was the dearly beloved son – or daughter – of somebody? Or 'Suffer the little children to come unto me'? It looked so bleak, so – unloved.

Thinking of this depressed her. She decided to go back to the house and begin telling her story. In her room she plugged in the microphone. She hesitated. How to begin? She drew a deep breath, and switched on.

'Dear Mum, this is me, Minty,' she began. 'And I'm going to tell you a story. It's a true story, of what's happening to me here at Belton, and it's absolutely secret. Only you in the whole world will ever hear it.' She paused, then smiled. 'Are you lying comfortably? Then I'll begin . . .'

And so she began to tell her story, starting at the beginning with the strange words that World had said to her when they first met. She told everything, and as she did so the story shaped itself in her mind, she seemed to relive it, and time stood still.

'And that's all, for now,' she said at last to the unlistening tape. 'You'll have to wait for the next instalment. Who is the mysterious hooded child? And why is she seen only at night? And who is the sinister Miss Raven, the ghost-hunter . . .?'

She switched off the machine. She sat for a moment, then turned it on again.

'And I've been thinking . . . Moontime – that's where I think *you* are, at the moment . . . somewhere away in moontime . . . So perhaps you'll understand better than I think. Goodbye, Mother Goose, for now.'

But although the telling was finished Minty's mind went on puzzling, looking for clues.

'What happens to time, when the moon shines on a sundial . . .?'

The riddle persisted. She pictured the garden at night, lying quiet and bathed in silvery light. She saw the worn dial, with its curved beak silently marking the long watches of the night. Then she decided.

'I'll go tonight,' she thought, 'before that Raven woman gets here.'

She was filled with a strong excitement, and

remembered the voice of the hooded child singing out of the darkness.

'It's her I want to see!' she thought.

But the child had been young. If she were there again, she might take fright at the sight of Minty standing there in her strange clothes.

'I'll try and look as if I'm from her time,' she decided. 'I'll wear that long nightie, and my grey school duffel with the hood. It'll look like a cloak in that light.'

She was so seized by the scheme that she longed to share it, and was half-tempted to switch on the microphone again, and tell it.

'Better not,' she thought. 'Don't want to scare her. Tell her afterwards.'

'Come and give me a hand, Minty, please!'

Aunt Mary had been bothering about for hours now, arranging the house for her new guest. She was to have the small room almost opposite Minty's own.

'At least she can't see the church from there, or the house,' Minty thought. Then, aloud, 'Coming, Aunt Mary!'

'Just give me a hand moving this chest, dear,' Aunt Mary said. 'Then I'll have room to put that little table from the top of the stairs.'

'What for?'

'Because she'll want to write, dear. She's writing a book, remember. You can't sit writing at chests, you want something you can put your feet under. Do you think she'll like that picture? I fetched it out of the cupboard specially.'

'Lovely,' said Minty mechanically. She then actually looked at the picture, and her heart jumped. It was the moondial! It was painted in oils, dark and cracked with age, and framed in crumbling gilt.

Minty's mind raced. She could not bear to think of Miss Raven of the cold eyes sitting and staring at the picture, perhaps even sensing its power, guessing that it was the key that freed the children, let them loose in time.

'It – it's a bit shabby,' she said.

'Oh, that doesn't matter. It's old, remember. She likes old things.'

'There – there's the old photos in my room,' Minty said. 'She could have those. And I'd have that instead. I wouldn't mind.'

'Oh, I've already shown her those,' Aunt Mary said.

'She's been in my room?' Minty was horrified.

'She was very interested in them,' Aunt Mary continued. 'Though I do wish you'd keep your room a little tidier, dear.'

'Sorry! I didn't realize it was open to visitors!' The words were out before she could stop them.

'That, Minty, was not an overly polite thing to say,' Aunt Mary said, after a pause. 'But I shall make allowances, under the circumstances.'

The pair of them moved the furniture and the picture stayed where it was.

'Where did you say Miss Raven was from?' Minty asked casually as they worked.

'Oh, she didn't say. I had the impression that she travelled about a good deal. "Here, there and everywhere!" she said.'

Minty did not like the sound of this. That Miss

Raven should have no fixed abode made her all the more tricky and hard to pin down.

When the guest room was arranged to Aunt Mary's liking Minty went back to her own room and sat on the bed.

'Look, Araminta Cane,' she told herself, 'I'm going to give you a good talking to!'

This was something she did from time to time, when there seemed a need. It was something Kate had taught her to do. She said that she did it herself.

'It helps to get things clear,' she said.

'Now listen,' Minty told herself. 'That Miss Raven is probably the most harmless old duck in the world. You haven't even met her yet. She probably sits crocheting egg cosies for Bring and Buys when she's not looking for ghosts. She probably has a hot water bottle, and wears lace-up shoes like Miss Waters.'

She rummaged in her mind for further proofs of harmlessness.

'And she probably wears thermal vests and has a cup of cocoa at bedtime.'

She was not deterred by the seasonal unlikelihood of these last two items. They even led her, by association, to further thoughts.

'*And* breaks the ice on the bird bath, and puts out fat for the tits.'

She nodded, satisfied.

'Just a dear old lady,' she said, 'a harmless old bat,' and resolutely dismissed the whole matter. It was a device that had worked well in the past. She turned her mind to the practical details of tonight's adventure. How exactly was she to get out of the house? Did Aunt Mary lock the house at night? If so, where did she put the keys?

'This is delicious trifle,' she told Aunt Mary at teatime. 'Do you lock up the house at night?'

'What a question! As if I wouldn't! You never know who's about – even in the daytime.'

'I thought you probably did,' Minty said. 'I just thought I'd make sure.'

'You've no need to worry your head about that at all, dear,' Aunt Mary told her. 'I lock the doors, front and back, every night. And then I take the keys out and hide them in a safe place. You have to do that, because otherwise a burglar could get in through a window, then unlock the door from the inside, and take away every stick of furniture in the house.'

She had clearly given the matter thought.

'Good thinking!' said Minty, and waited hopefully.

'So I put the keys every night in the tea caddy,' finished Aunt Mary, gratified by Minty's approval.

'Brilliant!' said Minty. And 'Thanks!' she added silently.

All she had to do now was wait. The evening seemed endless. She wandered out into the street and saw a group of children by the Post Office. They saw her and stared. Minty walked past them.

'I'm the one who's new here,' she thought. 'It's up to them to speak to me first.'

After she had passed she heard them whispering and giggling.

'Let them!' she thought. 'I've got other fish to fry!'

But she was careful to make sure they had gone before she walked back again.

Minty went to bed at nine o'clock. She closed the door of her room behind her and began her preparations with all the carefulness of a ritual. She took from a drawer the one long nightdress she had. This was one that had been given to her by Aunt Mary herself, who had no idea what the young wore in bed.

'Never thought *this* would ever come in useful!' she thought as she pulled it over her head.

She opened the wardrobe and found her long grey duffel coat.

'My cloak.'

She laid it carefully under the bed.

'Now – torch!'

She could not find it, though she felt certain she had brought it. In the end she decided that it did not matter. It might even be cheating to venture into moonlight, moontime, with her own private source of artificial light.

She went to the window and looked out. Her

eyes went to the church tower, where the gilt pennants caught the last brightness of the sun. Soon she would see them under another, colder light. Her way into the garden would be through the tall, wrought-iron gates dividing it from the graveyard. She would take a deep breath before entering the graveyard, then march along the path, looking to neither left nor right for fear of gliding spirits, misty shapes. Not, she reminded herself, that there was any need to be afraid of ghosts. She had always known they were there, and was now actually on terms with one, and becoming fond of him.

'I'm coming!' she whispered.

Then she got into bed and checked her alarm. She did not think it likely that she would fall asleep, but as a safeguard set it for half past eleven. She meant to be in the garden for the high noon of the night – midnight. She read for a while, then put out the light and lay feigning sleep. Aunt Mary would be making her nightly round at half past ten. She would switch off all the lights, lock both doors and put the key in the tea caddy, then mount the stairs and check on Minty before going to her own room.

Minty had worked herself into slow, peaceful breathing by the time the door clicked softly open and she sensed Aunt Mary standing over her.

'Bless her!' came a soft whisper. Then, after a pause, the click of the door and creaks along the landing.

The last hour of waiting was the longest of all. Minty lay and tried to think calm and peaceful thoughts, but could feel her limbs twitching with impatience. Which was strange, because when she did finally get out of bed, at precisely half past eleven, they all at once seemed weak, particularly her legs.

'Come on, legs!' she told them. 'Stiffen up! You're going, whether you like it or not!'

She was shivering, too, despite the warmth of the night, and was glad of the thick enveloping duffel.

Softly she opened the door, then listened. She stepped on to the landing and just as carefully closed the door behind her. She began the tiptoe journey down the stairs into the hall and heard only the ticking of the clocks, insisting on the forward march of time, left right left right. Then the groping passage to the kitchen in almost moonless dark because the curtains were drawn against the night and its prowlers. The tea caddy was not hard to find. In this house, everything had its place – its exact place.

She opened the tin. There was a strong scent of tea, and then her fingers were diving in amongst the dry leaves, feeling for metal. She withdrew the two keys, took the smaller one and replaced the other.

She made the journey back among the dark, silent shapes of furniture that seemed strangely shrouded, as if in dust sheets.

Breath held, she groped for the lock of the door, found it, and inserted the key. It turned easily.

'Remember to click up the latch!' she told herself.

Then the door was closed, ever so softly, and she was out in the night. The air was still and quite warm, as if the sun that had baked the earth and stones all day was now releasing its heat. There was a heavy scent of roses, grass clippings and privet.

The moon, almost full, hung huge and motionless, high in the sky. Minty looked up at it and drew a long, shuddering sigh. All about it lay faint Stardust, light years away.

The familiar walk down the path and along the road to the church gate seemed like a journey in a foreign land under that unaccustomed light. Even the quality of the silence was different. It was so absolute that she felt she must hold her breath.

But as she went the moon seemed to grow and give off such brilliance that she would not have been surprised if the birds had started to sing. It seemed light enough for a lark, even.

She was at the gate of the churchyard. The tall slabs, crosses, praying angels, lay washed in a calm and pallid light. They looked oddly self-contained and formal, less higgledy-piggledy now than under the sun. They seemed more certainly to spell death.

'I'll walk, not run, straight down the path. I'll look straight ahead. I won't think.'

Minty pulled up the hood of her duffel to blinker her vision and stepped into the graveyard. The daytime smell of dry yew was gone. She smelled cold green odours, strong and damp. As she passed the corner by the tower the iciness flowed past her like a stream. Almost there. There!

The tall wrought-iron gates were shut. Minty lifted the latch and pushed it, but it would not give.

'Locked! Oh no – no!'

It was something she had not even thought of. She scanned about, desperate, because she had fixed her heart on the moondial and midnight.

'Yeeeow!'

She let out a little shriek and whirled round in time to see the long lean curve of a cat melt into the shadows to her left. She stared after it. That way, if any, was the one she must take, down the edge of the graveyard, a high stone wall dividing it from the gardens. To her right gleamed the orangery, watery and insubstantial, a mere reflection.

'If I go along the edge of the graveyard,' she thought, 'I might get to a part of the wall that's broken down. Or that has something nearby that I could climb on to, to get up.'

By 'something' she meant a grave, but kept the thought pushed away. It had been no part of her plan to walk over graves, let alone use one as a mounting block.

She walked to the far side of the church and saw that already the path had given out. She would have to weave her own way between the graves. As she stood hesitating she glimpsed a pale shape winding through the long grass.

'Another cat!'

She scanned about her.

'Puss!' she whispered. 'Puss!'

But at night cats come into a mysterious kingdom of their own. The proud king cat, with shuttered eye, walks in his own and private light.

She went on, the solitary human in that cat-haunted place. She glimpsed a large ginger, moon-bleached, then a shabby grey. She wondered whether they came there every night, and even whether they were real. Could she have stumbled on the ancient mystery of the cat? Could it be that the cat exists not by the death-dealing rule of the clock but by moontime?

'Every cat has nine lives . . .' The saying seemed all at once deeper, and Minty found herself translating it, 'Every cat has nine moon lives.'

The thinking of these thoughts had brought her to the very middle of the churchyard. She moved her gaze past the gliding cats and leaning stones to the wall.

There, at the far end, as she had half known there would be, was the gap she needed.

To reach it she had to wade knee-high in grass and nettles. She saw with relief that the stones that had crumbled would give her a foothold. She would not have to climb wittingly on to a gravestone. The opening was in fact a kind of window into a small stone shelter, a tiny summerhouse.

She scrambled up and was poised for a moment on the shattered wall. She looked behind her and was aware of glassy eyes. Ahead she saw the path that would take her to the moondial. She lifted her skirts and jumped. She was in the dank, stone-smelling house. Then she was out in the garden itself.

'Now you've done it, Araminta Cane!'

Her tryst with the moondial was only minutes away now. She moved towards it, aware of the shadows and the absolute windless hush. An owl called and the sound echoed as if far away in a tunnel.

Then for the first time she saw that strange

ill-matched pair of wrestling figures by moonlight. Slowly she walked round them, awed by their beauty in that chill, piercing light. It feathered their wings and tipped the curls of the cherubic boy. He seemed, despite his blind eyes, to be smiling.

'Silver suits him,' she thought.

Then, reluctantly, she looked at the man, and noted fearfully the straining sinews, the sheer power and mastery of him. She raised her eyes and saw that his hair and beard were silvered but that his eyes were black holes.

'Who are you?' she breathed.

And then the church clock began to strike the hour.

'I must look at the dial! See where the shadow falls!'

But already the shift of time had begun. She was drawn irresistibly into the turn of seasons and could hear the lost voices. As if she were drowning, she snatched at straws of sights and sounds, but the whirlpool dragged her into its dark centre.

There was sudden peace. Minty stood swaying, then opened her eyes.

'Still night!'

It was still night and still moonlight. The owls in the tunnels hooted about her and nothing had changed except time itself. She looked up at the different stars and marvelled that she should witness them. Slowly she wheeled about, scanning the deserted garden. Perhaps, she thought, she must herself make the first move in this elaborate game that seemed to have no rules. Fearfully she looked towards the great moon-washed face of the house and took a few faltering paces forward.

She paused, then set off again. She was walking, after all, on a familiar path. She knew those clipped yews, those stone plinths with their wreathed flowers and fruit.

'Quick! Here!'

Minty stopped dead. She listened. There was a sound of muffled laughter, surely children's laughter? It was somewhere to her right.

'Sssssh!'

Minty, unnerved by the whispers from invisible mouths, stepped swiftly from the path and behind one of the plinths. She crouched low, half-kneeling on the damp grass, and waited. She heard no more, and yet had a strong sense that she was not alone, that others, too, were watching and waiting. It was as if the whole garden were waiting, breath held.

Then, very faintly, there came the sound of a child's voice singing. Minty felt the hair at the nape of her neck stir.

> *'Poor Mary sits a-weeping, a-weeping,*
> *a-weeping,*
> *Poor Mary sits a-weeping on a bright*
> *summer's day . . .'*

It was as if the moonlight made its own echoes. The voice rang pure and clear as if carried in frost.

She edged forward and saw the small cloaked figure moving over the moon-bathed terrace towards the seven steps down into the garden. The

139

child reached them and came on down them and as she came she sang.

'Soon I shall see her face,' Minty thought.

Now, as before, the song changed.

> *'Girls and boys come out to play*
> *The moon doth shine as bright as day . . .'*

Now Minty saw the others. The garden was filled with them. They moved out of the shadows from all directions, silently assembling as if at a secret signal. She knew without turning her head that they were behind her, too.

The child, oblivious, still came on singing. She was almost level with the yew where Minty was hidden.

Minty felt fear thicken in her throat. It was too late now to step out, she would be directly in the child's path. She stared helplessly as the small figure trailed past, face hidden by the curving folds of the hood. Then she looked again at the assembling host of listeners, advancing now, stealthily, over the

bleached lawns. Suddenly aware of a presence, she looked over her shoulder and her hand flew up to stifle a scream.

Horrorstruck she watched the figure, also that of a child, creep towards the path to cut off retreat to the house.

The figure had no face! It was wearing a loose sack over its head and hanging down to its waist. There were two gaping holes in it, like the cavernous eyes of a skull. Minty shuddered. Beyond the path she saw that the other advancing figures were all similarly shrouded. They closed in with slow menace.

The singing girl had reached the moondial now and stood gazing up at it, all unaware. As she did so the hood slipped and fell to her shoulders and Minty could see her bare head, hair hanging pale and straight.

'Who *are* you?' she heard the girl say, and shivered to hear her own earlier words echoed.

'Secret, you are . . .' the child continued. 'Seem it, to me. Perhaps because I only see you at night . . .'

She stood gazing up, and was so rapt and dreaming that she seemed not to hear the soft, whispering chant that now set up from the shrouded watchers.

'What time is it, Mr Wolf ... what time is it, Mr Wolf ...?'

With each repetition of the question the dark shapes and their shadows took a long stride forward.

'Surely she hears them?'

Minty was torn between a desire to warn her, and terror of the masked army with holes for eyes.

'I know you're really a sundial,' she heard the girl say, 'but not to me. I've got a clock to tell the daytime – tick tock tick tock ...'

'Tick tock tick tock!' breathed a mocking chorus behind her.

'To me you're not a sundial – you're a moondial!'

Minty's very bones seemed to melt as she heard the words.

'Moondial, moondial ...' echoed the whispers.

Then, suddenly changing rhythm, a new chant.

'Devil's child! Devil's child! Devil's child!'

The voices were gathering now in power, loud, insistent.

'Devil's child! Devil's child!'

Now at last the child did hear, and she whirled about to face her tormentors, and gave a little terrified whimper and pulled up her hood.

The ring of children stood fixed now, motionless. There was a little silence. Then the calling began, each voice from behind its muffling sack.

'Ware the devil's daughter!'

'Stay where you are!'

'She's got the Eye – the Evil Eye!'

'No – I'm not! I haven't! Oh please!'

The child stood terrified and shrinking. Both hands clutched at her hood as if for protection.

'My ma says so – she's seen her!'

'She's got the devil's mark!'

'Look at her – hiding it!'

'Frit we'll see it!'

'Devil's child, devil's child, devil's child!' The chant set up again first here, then there, until at last they all joined in. The gaping-eyed figures started to advance again.

'No!' screamed the child, and in her scream was pure terror. She cowered back, pressed against the statue.

'No!' And Minty found herself rushing headlong into the nightmare. How she reached her she did not know, but she found herself there by the moondial, her arms around that little muffled figure, holding her tightly. She could feel the hard thud of the child's heart, like that of a terrified animal. She turned, facing the attackers.

'No!' she cried again, and heard her own voice go ringing away through the moonlit acres until it died into silence. She felt the younger child clinging, and whispered:

'It's all right! You're safe with me!'

No one moved. The whole black and silver garden stood in tableau. Minty could hear a whispering among the wavering hollow-eyed shapes.

'Who is it, who is it? A ghost! What?'

Minty sensed their fear and with sudden

inspiration she released the child, raised her arms and advanced purposefully towards them.

'I am Araminta Cane!' she intoned. 'And I have come for you!'

'A ghost! A ghost!'

'Wheee!' Minty wailed. 'I'm coming, I'm coming! Wheee!'

They shrieked and scattered. Some tore off their sacks and fled, others stumbled and lurched after them, half-blinded by their own disguise. They knocked against the stone plinths, fell sideways into bushes, zigzagged drunkenly over the silvered lawns.

'Whooooo! Wheeeeee!'

It was marvellous! They had come intently, stalking like hunters, and now they ran pell-mell, head over heels almost. The night was a sudden scatter of shadows, then shivered back into calm again. Minty laughed with relief and elation. She had said 'Boo!' to the goose! Those sinister hooded figures were only silly children, now scared half out of their own wits.

Her arms fell to her sides. She remembered the other terrified child, but even as she turned that same shrill voice as before rang out.

'Sarah! Sarah! Where are you!'

Minty whirled again. A tall, dark figure was approaching rapidly, along the terrace, down the shallow steps.

'And what was that commotion! Sarah! Do you hear me!'

'Oh please, please!'

Minty heard the desperate cry behind her. As the woman sped towards them she held out her arms, prepared to act ghost again. But the woman was level with her, skirts swishing, had passed her, had seized the terrified child and was shaking her.

'Wicked child! What have I told you?'

'Don't – please don't! I didn't—'

The woman had her by the arm and began to drag her back towards the house.

'Stop!' Minty cried, and stepped into her path. She had a glimpse of a cold white face and heard the hiss:

'Devil's child! That's what you are! Devil's child! Back where you belong!'

Minty fell back, astounded. The woman had neither seen nor heard her.

'No!' she cried again. 'Stop!'

The child's head turned, but the hood turned with it.

Minty ran after them. She tugged at the woman's cape, but even as she did so knew how it would be.

'Stop! Stop!' her own voice was only an echo, her empty fingers spread while the long black winds of time streamed by, bearing her helplessly back to another night, the one she had set out from.

FIVE

No morning had ever been stranger than the one that followed. In her dreams Minty had been pursued by faceless shapes and their whispering chant, 'Devil's child, devil's child, devil's child!'

Now in daylight she tried to make some meaning of it all. She wondered why the hooded children had stalked the moonlight for the girl they had called by that terrible name. Who was the child who had no friends, who played alone in the darkness and kept her face hidden?

At the beginning, World had talked of the children crying, begging to be set free. Tom, she was sure, was one of them. But it was Sarah, imprisoned twice over – by night, and by that tall white-faced woman in black – whose cries for help must be carrying over the wastes of time to haunt World, and now herself.

'I'll set her free,' Minty told herself. 'I absolutely swear I will.'

She wanted to do it immediately, at that very moment. But she had hours of twentieth-century daylight between her and the next darkness. She was divided from Sarah by a barrier of sunlight.

'You won't be late at dinnertime, will you, dear?' said Aunt Mary at breakfast. 'Miss Raven will be here.'

'All right.' Minty smiled at her, happy in the knowledge that she had raided the tea caddy by night, locked and unlocked doors, come and gone as she pleased.

'And I'll do it again,' she thought. 'In and out like a ghost!'

She went out as soon as she had tidied her room in case of inspection by the public. She retraced her night-time steps, as if by doing so she could catch some hint or clue that had escaped her then.

It did not work. The sunshine and the colours distracted her. Hollyhocks that had been smoky

150

columns were now insistent pinks and reds and yellows. The dark sky, smudged with star-frost, was now a bright unsecretive blue.

The graveyard itself was sunlit, owlless. She gazed at the headstones, barnacled and tipsy as if washed up by the tide. She walked intently as any beachcomber on the high and dry line of the shore. The little icy tongues of wind licked her face by the corner of the tower. They were a consolation, a sign that things were not as they seemed.

Instead of taking the approved path through the iron gates she turned left, and waded through long grass towards the break in the wall. Ahead of her she saw a large ginger cat paddling its way towards the sunshine and a warm slab. She had forgotten the cats.

'Puss!' she called. 'Puss!'

The cat turned and looked with his ellipitcal amber eyes. Then, tail erect, he continued on his way, brushing her off. She was affronted.

'*I* know about moontime, too!' she called after him.

But on he trod, and the grasses flattened and lifted again like waves in his wake.

She had reached the ruined window that had been her entry to the garden.

'It's still there, then!'

She had not really doubted it. But the events of the night had taken on such a curious, dreamlike quality that it seemed altogether possible that the wall had fallen away before her, and had now closed up again, like a thicket.

She scrambled up and dropped to the other side. She enjoyed the sensation of entering the garden by her own secret entrance. It put her into a different category from the law-abiding passers through proper gates and entrances. She had always seen herself as the possessor of secrets. A secret, any secret, was a source of power. She did not put this idea into words, it was simply an instinct she had.

She looked down at her jeans and brushed away the damp leaves that were clinging to them, and as she did so caught sight of silvery trails, bright in the shadows. That was another thing, she thought.

You only ever saw snail tracks in the morning. That meant that they, too, were creatures of the moon, however unlikely it might seem. She found it hard to bracket snails with owls, bats, cats. On the other hand, she had always been fond of them, and remembered trying to keep them as pets when she was very little. She had tried to house them in empty egg boxes and plastic buckets, and had brought them fancy food – snapdragon heads, dandelions and rose petals, sometimes even biscuits. She had given them names like Dawdle and Lucy, and had cried when she had found them gone by morning. For hours on end she had patiently unravelled their silvery threads about the garden, but all she ever seemed to find were empty shells, often broken.

'Good old snails!' she thought now. 'They *do* live by moontime – must!'

She walked slowly, enjoying her solitary possession of the garden. The early mornings and the evenings, with their long shadows and echoing birdsong, were times when anything could happen, on the fringe of moontime itself. She would not have been altogether surprised to see the old sack-hooded straggler from the night before.

She thought of Sarah and wondered where she was now. Somewhere in the great, many-roomed House, she guessed, a prisoner, guarded by that woman in black. She, too, had called Sarah 'devil's child'. What could she mean – devil? A wicked lord, perhaps, who had committed some crime … but then … what was the 'devil's mark' they had spoken of …?

She had reached the moondial, and her mood had changed. She felt an unbearable sadness for that lonely night child, and despair at ever rescuing her.

'How *can* I?' she asked out loud.

But she had promised – promised World, and herself. She gazed at the stone wrestlers and again thought how unequal the struggle was, how vainly the small winged boy fought. On impulse she put out a hand and touched him lightly on his stone curled head.

'I'm on your side!' she whispered.

It was as if she had found a secret touchstone to make time itself dissolve. She went floating into a strange slow dance of seasons, in which she felt rather than saw light wheeling in huge arcs, she herself at their centre. In rapid succession she smelled woodsmoke, glimpsed snowdrops, blackberries, felt rain slanting on her cheeks, heard a cuckoo call. And beyond there were the voices, whispering, pleading, crying.

The dance slowed and the voices faded. Silence. A huge, enfolding snow silence. Soft cold stings on face and arms. Cold.

Minty opened her eyes. She gasped and blinked, dazzled by the mazy flakes that swarmed like great white bees about her. She could see nothing else, not a single landmark. She might have been adrift in space as well as in time.

'Winter!'

Stretching her arms before her as if playing Blind Man's Buff, she moved falteringly forward. She did not want to lose the anchor of the moondial. Even at home and in her own time, to walk alone in so dense and swirling a snow-shower was to be cut off from the whole world, isolated. She remembered moments of panic in the past when she had had the nightmarish conviction that everyone and everything had vanished forever.

'I could get lost,' she thought fearfully. Then, 'No – I can follow my own footprints back!'

Flooded with relief at the inspiration, she turned her head and looked down for the visible reassurance of the steps she had already taken.

'Oh – no!'

She stared in disbelief at the blank surface of the snow behind her. There were no footprints.

Her head reeled with terror, as if she had found herself on the edge of an abyss. Her very existence seemed threatened.

'This is how it feels to be a ghost!'

Panic-stricken now and shivering, she stumbled back towards the moondial. She could not see it, but only guess at its direction.

Then, faintly, she heard the voices of children.

She began to hurry towards them, longing for human contact in this enveloping whiteness. At last she could make them out, blurred shapes, seven or eight of them. She stopped and watched. They were making a snowman.

'That's it! That's got her!'

'Now the cloak!'

'Give us the cloak, Sam!'

One boy picked up a bundle lying nearby, shook it out and began to drape it round the snowman. Except that it was a snowgirl. Now she knew what they were doing.

'Pull it up, right over, like she does!'

Now the snow figure stood fully cloaked and hooded. The effect was uncanny. It could have been Sarah herself.

Satisfied, the children fell back. Then as if by common consent they started to prowl about the effigy in a ring, and one by one they joined in the whispered chant:

'Devil's child, devil's child, devil's child!'

A boy stopped, and scooping up a snowball

hurled it at the dark figure. It struck the hood, and the rest yelled with delight and followed suit.

Minty, watching invisible behind the curtain of snow, knew that what they were doing was the same as sticking pins into a wax image. Horrified, she saw the figure lean and topple.

'Hurrah!'

'Dead! Dead! Dead!'

They rushed forward and began to knock down what was left of the snow, kicking it, jumping up and down on it. Soon it had disappeared, the cloak lay limp and empty, sprawled like a dead black bird.

Minty turned and stumbled away, sickened, trying to blot out their shrieks. Gradually the voices faded and she was again in that huge snow silence, no man's land. By now she was hopelessly lost, but kept going because she had no other choice. To stop would be to invite that thing she had heard of, when travellers yielded to the temptation to stop, to sink into the soft, alluring snow.

Now and then she lurched blindly into the trunks

of trees, and hopelessly tried to read their knots and whorls, touching them with her fingers before reeling off again into the void. It seemed as though hours passed.

At last she came to a different tree, fully leaved and solid, and knew that it was one of the giant yews that stood sentinel at the entry to the formal garden. She leaned against it, half-sobbing with relief, and felt the snow from its leaves slither about her.

Now she was only a few yards away from the moondial and safety. She moved off slowly, straining her eyes into the mazy flakes for its outline. It seemed to her that now the fall was not so heavy, that the air was brightening.

Then she heard a familiar, racking cough.

'Can't be,' she thought. 'Sarah's time, this is, not his!'

But Tom too could travel back in time, he had seen Sarah even before Minty herself. Staggering forwards, arms outstretched like a sleepwalker, she dimly made out a figure. It was Tom. He was stamping his feet, clapping his arms about his chest, and evidently had not seen her.

'Take a big breath – in! Let it go – out!'

He snuffed mightily. He was doing the breathing exercises that would make him six feet tall and a footman in blue and silver livery. She watched the brave figure stamping and snuffing, and noticed how his thin wrists poked from the sleeves of his ragged jacket, the gap of bare flesh between breeches and clumsy boots.

'Tom!' she called, and plodded towards him.

By now he was racked by coughs again, bent double. As she reached him he finally straightened up and saw her.

'Oh!' He was still wheezing for breath. 'You again!'

'Tom! What's happening? Why is it snowing?'

He stared, disgusted.

'Oh, Old Mother Goose, ain't it, shaking her feathers down from the sky! Why d'you *think* it's snowing!'

'No, what I meant—' she broke off. It was too

much to explain. She must let her time go, live in this present.

'Thought you was never coming. Where've you *been*?'

She did not answer the question. She did not know, any more than he did.

'How – how's Dorrie?' she asked.

'She's poorly, ain't she? Coughing, like me. What d'you expect, gutter-picking? Why d'you think I'm out here, freezing? Hey – have I grown – have I?'

Minty looked at the thin figure, the stooping shoulders and blue wrists.

'Definitely,' she said. 'A lot!'

'Wheee! Knew I had!' he cried triumphantly. He danced and kicked the snow with his boots to make his own private shower. He was shuddering with cold and so, now, was she.

'Tom, you're frozen! You'll catch your death of cold, out here in those clothes. Here – come with me! You must get warm!'

'Warm – what? Where? Where's the fire? *I* don't see no fire!'

'No, not a fire. Here! Come on!'

She seized him by the wrist and began to tug him in the direction she had come from. At the time she did not know why, she simply did it. She strained into the lazily falling flocks of snow and made out the shape of the moondial.

'Here!' she said, and her own teeth were chattering.

She groped for the snow-capped head of the winged boy.

'Help us!' she cried.

The pair of them went, hand in hand, into the light, down the long corridors of sunlight and the warm blowing winds.

This time, when the sudden silence and stillness came and Minty opened her eyes, she was not alone. She saw Tom's startled face, inches away from her own.

'Oh lawks!' he exclaimed. 'It *is* warm!' and he spread his fingers to the sun as if to a fire. 'Hey – you! How did you do it?'

Silently she pointed to the moondial.

'Oh yes. I know *that*. But how did you know for sure? Times I've tried, and nothing's happened!'

'I know,' she agreed. 'But I think it's him.'

He followed her pointing finger.

'What? The little 'un?'

She nodded.

'But why? He ain't even winning – can't! Look at the size of him, against the big feller! Bet *he* could be a footman, if he stood up straight! Bet he's seven foot, let alone six!'

'It was the boy,' Minty insisted.

He shrugged, then made a mock salute towards the figure.

'Thanks then, Charlie!'

Minty laughed.

'Charlie! Why d'you call him that?'

'Dunno. My pa's name, that is. Was.'

'Oh.' She said nothing more. She did not want to be reminded of dead fathers. He was looking about him, his old self, quite thawed out.

'This your time?'

'Yes.' She had checked the chimneys of the

House, but without really needing to. She knew in her bones that this was the selfsame morning she had left only minutes ... years ... centuries earlier.

'Think I'll stop,' he said. 'In fact, if I could fetch Dorrie here, I would for sure.'

Then his face was suddenly puzzled.

'There's a funny thing ...' he said.

'What?'

'Dorrie. You know that kind of tunnel you go through, with the wind blowing?'

She nodded.

'Them voices. Just now, when we came through. I could've sworn I heard her. Calling my name, she was.'

His face brightened.

'Here – what if she's here?' He scanned eagerly about the still-deserted garden.

'Could be! She'd be hiding, sure enough, little monkey. Dorrie! Dorrie!'

He turned to Minty.

'Come on – let's find her!'

He went, darting between the stone plinths and the Christmas-pudding bushes, playing a private game of hide and seek with an imaginary quarry. Minty followed, humouring him.

'Wait!'

When she caught up with him his face was flushed, his eyes were bright.

'The grotto!' he said. 'Sure as sixpence she'll be there, in among them old rocks!'

He was off again, along the terrace, through the passage, across the courtyard.

'Coming!' he yelled. 'Watch out!'

He was making for the wild, wooded side of the main drive, down by the river.

'The adventure playground,' Minty thought. 'Did he say grotto?'

By the time she herself had crossed the wooden bridge over the narrow stream, Tom had vanished. She looked about her. She had not yet explored here, though she had glimpsed children scaling the timber frames, scrambling high among the branches. She had meant to come here often, make friends, perhaps. But now she had met other children, had an adventure of her own. This, she thought, was only playing at adventure, a game to pass the time.

'Tom!' she shouted. 'Where are you?'

But he was playing a game of hide and seek with herself as well as his sister. Not that Minty believed for a moment that Dorrie was anywhere here. She set off in search of him. As she went she was aware of the curious, ancient feel of the place. There were huge rocks and boulders that might have been rolled there by giants. The trees themselves were oddly unEnglish, with massive silvery or reddish trunks, fantastically whorled and scarred. Beneath her feet was a dense, spongy layer of loam.

There was a sudden quick shiver of the foliage ahead.

'I see you!' called Minty, and saw that it was not Tom at all, but a young deer, golden-brown and shining. It leapt across the clearing and had vanished into the greenery, leaving a glitter of shaking leaves.

She was enchanted by the swift visitation. It struck her as a kind of sign.

'Minty!'

She shaded her eyes to look upwards into a blinding shaft of sunlight. There sat Tom on a log-tree platform, legs and lumpy boots dangling.

'Who's a dirty rascal?'

She laughed and darted forward to find the way up to join him, to be joint king of the castle. By the time she got there he was gone again.

Perhaps he had learned to lurk and dodge in the smoky alleys of London. Pursuits along narrow gutters and even over rooftops and among chimneys might have been the stuff of life to him. A wily town fox, now in the country, he twisted and turned, now here, now there. The wood was scattered with his laughter.

At length Minty, breathless, dropped on to a fallen log.

'Give up!' she gasped, and then, more loudly, 'Give up!'

She would wait and let him come to her. As she

sat, the silence in the wood deepened. She heard the whistle of birds, the distant tap tap of a woodpecker and the refrain of running water. But now there was not the least rustle or crack that might betray Tom's presence.

He must be there somewhere, she told herself. But she grew uneasy. If he were scrambling up ladders, swinging from boughs, he might have fallen. He might be lying hurt, even unconscious. If he had hurt himself, how would he reach the moondial? Her thoughts raced. Say he had broken a leg – what then? How could an ambulance with its white-coated men and flashing blue lights rescue a boy from a century ago? In any case, she reminded herself, he would be invisible to them.

Even if she managed to help him all that way back to the garden, and he went back to his own time, how would he fare? Would it still be snowing? She pictured Tom lying hurt in the snow, clad only in his thin jacket and breeches. She thought of the terrible Maggs and the badgering, unmotherly Mrs Crump, and shuddered.

'Tom!' She stood up and called again, desperately now, angry with him. 'Tom! Come out this minute!'

But he wouldn't – or couldn't. Then she heard a new sound, one that she recognized, the sound of children being let out to play. Their shrieks and laughter were louder by the moment. Coachloads of children were rushing over to the river from the car park.

'Like a horde of savages!' she thought, echoing the phrase of countless teachers she'd known.

She reminded herself that Tom would be invisible to them, and almost in the instant her heart stopped in terror. These were children!

She remembered something World had said.

'Funny, children. Don't *know* a deal, but they see things more.'

She had a sudden vision of the moonlit garden and those hooded children swarming silently from the shadows.

'*They saw me!*'

And as those children had advanced on Sarah, so

she could see these children cornering poor Tom. She imagined him crouching back in terror as they surrounded him, taunting, mocking, pointing at his odd clothes and clumsy boots.

'Oh!' She was almost in tears. She stamped her foot.

Now she could see them, tumbling across the wooden bridge from the park, then running free into the trees with whoops and shrieks. Even she was afraid to be seen by them, they in a gang, she a stranger and alone. She ducked her head and ran, taking cover behind one of the outlandish crops of rock.

After an age the children had crossed the bridge, had scattered in all directions. Minty could hear their teachers' voices:

'Not too far, now!'

'All back here in fifteen minutes!'

She hesitated, uncertain what her next move should be.

Her best plan, she decided, would be to return to the moondial and wait. In the end Tom would find his way back there. He might be in a strange century, but the landmarks were all still there and still the same. The House had woken up for the day now, and there would be people about – guides, gardeners, stewards. But they were all adults. They would not see the daylight ghost of a small Victorian boy.

Her mind made up, she straightened, then went towards the bridge. There was a man in the wooden hut, counting tickets. He looked up and saw her but made no comment, and returned to his task. He probably thought she was one of the school party, returning to the coach for a forgotten camera, or sandwiches.

She was crossing the main drive when she heard her name called. Turning, she saw World, sitting wide-kneed on a chair in his doorway, sunning himself. He beckoned.

Minty hesitated. Should she or not? Minutes were precious. Then she saw that he had turned his head away, and was calling after another figure, walking away down the drive.

'Mary!' he heard. 'Mary! She's here!'

The figure turned.

'There you are!' came Aunt Mary's voice. 'Come along, I want you!'

Minty was trapped. She would have to go. Reluctantly she changed direction and went down the drive, waving fleetingly to World as she passed him.

'What luck, seeing you like that!' said Aunt Mary. 'I want you to come along back to the house with me, dear.'

'Oh! Now? Must I? I was just—' she broke off. It was not easy to invent important business in a garden.

'That nice Mr Benson rang, and he's going to call by to pick something up to take to your mother. He said you'd know what he meant.'

'Yes. Oh, yes.'

Aunt Mary was mercifully incurious. In any case, Minty reflected, she had probably never heard of cassettes.

'He said he'd be along in about an hour,' Aunt Mary told her.

'Which'll give me time to tell the second instalment,' Minty thought, letting go all thought of finding Tom now.

Up in her room she told of her midnight visit to the garden, of the children whose eyes were gaping holes in their sackcloth hoods, and the reappearance of the woman in black. Then, because Mr Benson still had not come, she brought the story up to date.

'And the worst of it is,' she ended, 'I don't know what's happened to him! Whether he's still in there, or he got back to his own time. But oh Mum, he was *freezing*, and you should hear him cough! And he's so lonely, and they're so cruel, that Maggs and Mrs Crump! And then there's his little sister Dorrie, and he says she's ill now, and coughing, just like him. They couldn't have got that awful thing you told me about – why you said there were so many children's graves in that time – what was it . . . consumption. Oh, they can't have got that, can they?'

She heard a car draw up, the toot of a horn.

'That's all for now. And I'll come in and see you tomorrow, and I want to see your eyes open! Are you listening? Lots of love ...'

She switched off the machine. By it was an envelope she had already labelled with bold black print: For Mrs K. Cane and STRICTLY CONFIDENTIAL. She hastily wrote CANE – TOP SECRET on the cassette itself, and put it in the envelope.

When she went down Aunt Mary was giving Mr Benson coffee.

'Hello, Minty. Got something for me?'

She handed him the envelope.

'You'll make sure no one else listens, won't you?' she begged.

'Don't worry. I will.'

'Some flowers would have been nice,' observed Aunt Mary.

'Not really,' said Minty. 'Not when she's got her eyes shut.'

'Flowers'll be fine when she's a bit better,' said Mr Benson.

'*Is* she getting better?' Minty asked. It now suddenly seemed to her that perhaps it was heartless of her to be so obsessed by the moondial. Perhaps she should be spending all her time at Kate's bedside. But in an obscure way she felt that her mother's own fate was bound up with the moondial, too.

'And Mum would want me to,' she thought. 'She wouldn't want me to be lonely. Or the others, either.'

Loneliness was the name of the game.

'Of course she's getting better,' Mr Benson said. 'It's just that it's happening in a way that you can't really see.'

'Invisibly,' said Minty. 'She's getting better invisibly.'

All the best things are happening invisibly at the moment, she thought.

'That's a funny word to use,' said Aunt Mary. 'I suppose she's still *there*.'

Minty, realizing that this was as close to being a joke as Aunt Mary would ever manage, made an effort to smile.

When Mr Benson went out to his car she ran after him.

'She *is* getting better, isn't she? You're not just saying it?'

He put his arm around her, and she liked that. Kate and she had always hugged a lot, and she had missed it. She smiled up at him, comforted.

'Good girl,' he said. 'Don't worry. She's coming back to us, slowly. And this,' he held up the envelope, 'will probably start showing on those screens the minute she hears it.'

'Really? Will it?'

For a moment she was half tempted to go along with him, to sit at Kate's bedside as she listened, and watch those wavering green lights on the screen. They might jump and leap, zigzag upwards. *That* would be visible!

'If it does, will you ring me up and tell me?'

'Course I will. Promise.'

He released her and went round the car. He opened the door, then paused.

'Lonely?' he asked.

She shook her head.

'But I miss Mum.'

He smiled at her.

'Not for much longer,' he told her, and got in.

Minty watched as he drove off towards the hospital and Kate, lying in the high white bed. She could feel the tears trapped painfully behind her eyes. Instead of going back to the house and Aunt Mary, she made for the churchyard, quickly, before the tears could spill.

She only just made it. As she went along the path by the church she was already half blinded. She passed through the stream of cold air by the tower and stumbled into the long grass beyond. There she found a large, sun-warmed headstone, and dropping to the ground she leaned against it and cried, partly for Tom who was an orphan and Sarah whose playground was the night, but most of all for herself, without Kate.

'I'm not being sorry for myself,' she told herself through the hot tears. 'I'm just having a good cry. It's good for you.'

When she had finished, found a tissue and dried her eyes, she did feel better. She looked up and saw, not more than a yard away, that same large ginger cat, watching her.

'Oh!' It was disconcerting to know that she had had an audience, even of only a single cat.

'Come on! Puss! . . . Oh well! You don't half *stare*!'

She had tried in the past to outstare cats, to gaze back at them unwinking till they had to look away. She never had, so did not bother trying now.

'Wouldn't be surprised,' she told the cat, 'if you were a scratcher! And biter!'

She got to her feet.

'I'm off! It's all yours!'

She indicated the whole sun-splashed graveyard, then turned and went.

As she went up the path to the cottage she saw that the door was standing open. She stepped into the shadowy hall and saw a large, black bag. There were voices from the sitting room. Minty walked in and saw Aunt Mary standing by the window with a tall, thin woman.

'Hello!' said Minty, and they both turned. At first she could not see their faces against the strong light.

'Here she is!' exclaimed Aunt Mary. 'Come along in, Minty, and meet our guest. This is Miss Raven.'

They both came towards her. Minty raised her eyes up past the black skirt and blouse, to see a long white face, hooded eyes.

'How do you do?' she said politely – and shivered.

Minty had to force the food down. She kept her eyes on the plate because that seemed safer than meeting the hard gaze of Miss Raven. Aunt Mary did not seem to notice.

'She doesn't even notice,' Minty thought, 'that Miss Raven's not listening to a single word she's saying.'

In the end, the visitor checked the flow of information about the old days at the House.

'And now,' she said, putting down her spoon, 'what about these ghosts?'

Minty held her breath, concentrated on her plate.

'Well, as to those,' said Aunt Mary, 'I'm afraid I can't help, as I told you. But there is some story about the Queen's Bedroom.'

'I shall go over there myself,' Miss Raven announced. 'I have a nose for ghosts.'

'Well, of course, if it's your *job*,' said Aunt Mary.

'And what about you, Araminta?' said Miss Raven softly. 'Perhaps you have seen something?'

'Oh, she's not been here five minutes!' said Aunt Mary.

'Children,' remarked Miss Raven, 'have to be watched. I often think of them as spies.'

'And she hasn't even been *in* the House yet,' went on Aunt Mary. 'Runs around in the garden all day, don't you, Minty?'

'Ah,' said Miss Raven. 'The garden.'

The silence was like a black hole.

'Then later, Araminta, you must show me the garden.'

'There!' said Aunt Mary. 'You hear that, Minty? I must say it does sound old-fashioned, Miss Raven, you calling her Araminta.'

'That is her name, is it not?' returned Miss Raven.

Minty herself was glad that this woman addressed her so formally, while at the same time wondering whether it was not sinister. Araminta, after all, was her real name. Perhaps in using it Miss Raven gained some extra power over her.

Lunch over, Aunt Mary organized the afternoon.

'I shall be in the shop till four,' she told the others. 'You and Miss Raven can walk over with me, Minty, and then you can show her the gardens.'

'I'm surprised at your allowing her to run all over, Mrs Bowyer,' said Miss Raven. 'In my day, children stayed put. You knew where they were.'

In her day, Minty thought, children were prisoners. She felt like one herself, forced to walk by the tall stiff woman with her creaking shoes.

World was pottering in his doorway as they passed. He watched wordlessly.

'Straight through that little door,' said Aunt Mary, as she left them.

The pair passed through the stone tunnel on to the terrace. Miss Raven stopped, looking about her. She drew a long sigh. Minty planned desperately how she might avoid going by the moondial.

'Look!' she cried, pointing to the left. 'The orangery! Shall we go there?'

'Along the terrace, I think,' replied Miss Raven.

They passed the calm, blank-eyed statues, and Minty wondered whether they were silently recognizing this visitor. She looked at them for clues. The stone eyes were fixed and expressionless. She felt, nonetheless, that they were witnesses.

'You seem a very silent child,' observed Miss Raven.

Minty could not think of a single thing in the whole world that she wished to say to Miss Raven. Except, of course, 'Go away!' Manners, unfortunately, forbade this.

Now that the silence had been remarked upon, Minty herself began to feel it awkward. And so, partly to fill that silence, and partly to hide her agitation as they descended the seven steps that led down towards the moondial, she began to hum under her breath.

'Don't!' said Miss Raven sharply.

Minty stopped.

They were passing between the golden

Christmas puddings and the stone plinths. In order to avoid looking ahead at the moondial itself, Minty examined each carving in turn. She had glanced at them before, and thought them rather uninteresting, just carvings of fruit and garlands of flowers. Now, with a slight shock, she saw a face, or rather a kind of stone mask with slit eyes, and had the unpleasant feeling that it was aware of her. She felt it sinister and mocking, and swiftly averted her eyes.

'Do you – feel anything?' asked Miss Raven. She stopped and looked down at Minty, her eyes hard and searching.

'Feel?' echoed Minty blankly. She put on what she hoped was an innocent expression.

'I – feel a bit hot . . .'

'I think you know what I mean,' said Miss Raven. 'Have you ever seen a ghost?'

'No!' lied Minty swiftly. 'Never!'

'That is strange,' said Miss Raven. 'I should have thought you were exactly the kind of child who did. *I* have . . .'

'It – must be very interesting,' said Minty. 'Aren't you scared?'

'Certainly not,' replied Miss Raven. 'Why should I be?'

'Most people would be.'

'I am not most people,' returned Miss Raven. 'I have special powers. And those powers tell me that now, at this very moment, there is some kind of . . . presence . . .'

'Where?' Minty looked all around and above her, as if trying to spot an aeroplane. 'I can't see anything.'

'I didn't say "see",' Miss Raven told her. She suddenly wrapped her black cardigan about her and shivered. 'Very strong . . .' she murmured. She looked ahead, at the statue, and began to move towards it.

'Oh!' she exclaimed. 'It's a sundial!'

Minty's own flesh was creeping.

'Is it?' she said casually, hoping that her voice did not tremble. 'I hadn't noticed.'

'How very interesting!' Miss Raven was

walking round it. 'What do the figures represent, I wonder?'

She stared hard at it, then gave herself a sudden shake.

'Come!' she said. 'Let us move on. Perhaps I am mistaken. One does not really expect a sundial to be haunted.'

Minty felt a rush of relief so powerful that she wanted to shout. They had passed through that moon-haunted, whispering circle, crowded with voices and glimpses of light like the flakes in a sunlit orchard. And Miss Raven had seen and heard nothing.

After that they walked to the orangery, and then Miss Raven noticed the church.

'I must see that,' she said. 'One can often gain very strong impressions in such places. I expect you think me very odd?'

'Oh, not at all,' lied Minty politely. 'Really I don't.'

Her attention was momentarily distracted by the quick flash of a black and white bird – a magpie.

Swiftly she scanned for another, but seeing none, saluted swiftly. The magpie flew into the dazzle from the glass of the orangery and vanished. Her companion seemed not to have noticed it. She certainly did not salute.

'If we go through the churchyard we'll be nearly home,' Minty offered as they approached the iron gates. She did not relish the thought of having to accompany Miss Raven back all the way they had come. Her very bones were now aching. She wanted to shake off the stiff and towering presence, to breathe again.

As they entered the graveyard the ginger cat appeared once more, threading the stones.

'Oh, look!' cried Miss Raven girlishly. 'What a beauty! Puss! Puss!'

The cat stood poised in mid tiptoe. He stared, separate and self-contained in his dense coat. He was isolated, wrapped in his golden fur, cat-years away.

'Puss!' coaxed Miss Raven again. 'Puss!'

Then, with carefully planted feet and swaying

tail, he came. Minty was amazed. Next minute Miss Raven had scooped him up and was cradling him in her arms. Minty stared at the pair, the long white face of the woman next to that of the secret, narrow-eyed cat.

'Witches have cats!' she found herself thinking.

Six

'Perhaps,' thought Minty, 'the moondial will take me wherever I ask it now.'

At first the moondial had been unpredictable, and Tom himself evidently found it so.

'Sometimes it don't work at all,' he'd said.

But now Minty felt that her power over it was growing. An appeal to the small winged boy would work the spell. After all he, too, was a child, locked in stone as the others were locked in time.

She wanted to pull the threads of her wandering in time together, to make a pattern of them, like a dance. There they all wandered in those long green avenues – Tom, Sarah, herself – without rhyme or reason. Now and again their paths crossed, they stumbled across one another, blind and aimless as bees in lavender. It could all go on forever. But Minty wanted to uncover a meaning. She sensed that it was there, pulling the three of them together, tugging them towards invisible ends.

'All three of us,' she thought. 'And we haven't even met – not all three of us together.'

And the thought of that meeting filled her with almost unbearable excitement.

'Because we all know each other, only separately,' she thought. 'Me and Tom. Me and Sarah. Tom and Sarah. We might only be one another's dreams.'

But if they were to meet face to face, all three, the reality of it would be plain and inescapable. And even if it were still a dream, what a dream it would be!

And so Minty began to move towards that meeting. She did not know how it would happen, only that it would. The world about her greened suddenly over like spring with her happiness. Even Miss Raven could not touch it.

'Perhaps, after tea, you would like to see my photographs,' she said.

Minty stared into her bowl of lime jelly as if into a

crystal ball, conjuring up a picture of a Miss Raven with a tall, pointed hat.

'That would be nice,' said Aunt Mary. 'Are they of your holidays?'

'I do not take holidays,' replied Miss Raven. 'They are a waste of time. These are of my work.'

'What – ghosts, you mean?' said Minty. 'Photos of ghosts? Oh yes, please!'

'Don't be silly, Minty,' Aunt Mary told her. 'We shall be ever so interested to see them, Miss Raven.'

The photographs were fetched, album upon album of them.

'I am an extremely keen photographer,' Miss Raven informed her audience. 'It has something to do with time, I think.'

'What?' Minty pricked up her ears at this.

'*Capturing* it,' said Miss Raven. 'Pinning down the passing second!'

'Like a butterfly?' suggested Minty.

'Exactly! In the instant the shutter clicks the instant is trapped! Think of it! Pinned forever!'

'That,' thought Minty, 'is what you think. Silly bat!'

She knew differently. She knew that time is fluid, watery beyond water even, because you cannot cup it in your hands however fleetingly.

'And it is the same thing, precisely, that excites me about ghosts!' said Miss Raven. She did indeed seem excited, cheeks flushed, voice eager.

'You mean you can pin them as well?' asked Minty.

'No! Because they are *already* pinned! Don't you see? Trapped in their past!'

Minty thought of Tom, running that morning through the trees under a bright hail of arrows of twentieth-century sunlight. It was in that moment she felt quite certain that Tom had reached home safely. If you could call it home.

'That,' she thought again, 'is what you think!'

'What interesting ideas,' said Aunt Mary, quite lost. 'Shall we look at the pictures then?'

Miss Raven opened the albums and proceeded to display moment upon dead, captured moment. Minty, watching her, thought:

'She is a jailer. She is trying to imprison time with her rotten camera. Now she's come here, and will try to imprison us, too. That's why she's come. She wants to capture Tom and Sarah, trap them in time, just like her horrible photos. But I'll stop her. That's why *I'm* here. I have the key – World said so . . .'

Minty was so certain of this that she did not plan to return to the garden that night. She felt tired, ready only for sleep and dreaming.

'Tomorrow will do,' she told herself, in the knowledge that as she fell asleep, so time would dissolve.

She woke early, and in the instant was ready for another journey. She reached for her clock. Just after five. As she pulled on her clothes she was shivering.

She opened her door with extreme care, mindful of the witch Raven opposite, deep in her dark dreams. It was only when she stepped outside the front door and clicked it gently behind her that she drew her first real breath.

The street was thinly washed with gold and the shadows were icy. A cockerel crowed from the farm beyond the church, tearing the dawn hush. The graveyard was drenched with dew and littered with cats, strayed from the night.

'Morning!' called Minty, splashing her way through them. 'Coming with me?'

She scrambled through the shattered stone window and was in the gardens. To her left the park, mile upon mile of it, rose from a low white bank of mist as if it were afloat. Minty looked down and was surprised that she could see her own feet.

'But I'm walking in it!' she said. 'Must be!'

That was something else invisible and yet there. She began to run, partly because it was cold but partly because she was excited by the certainty of things invisible and yet real. By the time she reached the moondial she was out of breath. She went straight to the winged boy and addressed him.

'It's me again,' she told him, 'Araminta Cane.' She paused. 'I know you can't tell me your name, but I know you've got one. And I'm going to find out what it is. But now ... now ... you know what I want, don't you ...?'

In that certainty she lightly touched his damp head and the stone melted under her fingers as she went gladly into the strange turning shift of time.

She came into a different dawn. Her eyes went automatically to the chimneys and their signals of smoke. There was no sign of Tom. Yet this, surely, must be his time? Sarah belonged to the night.

'Pssst! Minty!'

It was Tom. She looked vainly about her.

'Surely *he* can't have gone invisible?' she thought.

Then she saw him – or rather, part of him. He was behind one of the yews, and beckoning furiously. The bones of his wrists gleamed whitely.

'Quick! Here!' he whispered hoarsely.

Minty, mystified, obeyed.

'What's up? Maggs about?'

'Not 'im! Not even *born* yet, like as not!'

'*What?*'

As she spoke he reached and gripped her arm and pulled her beside him. She jerked away from him.

'What're you *doing*? What's up?'

'Ssshhh! Listen!'

195

Minty obeyed. Beyond the thudding of her own heart and Tom's rasping breath, she heard only the song of birds. A distant cuckoo called from the misty meadows beyond and marked the season as an earlier summer than the one she had left.

'In July, away I fly!' she thought.

She turned her head and looked at Tom, closer than she had ever seen him. His cheeks were scarlet, his lips parted.

'Why're we hiding?' she whispered. 'Who's after you?'

He shook his head.

'I came to fetch you,' she told him. 'I want us both to go to her together – Sarah. Come on – the moondial!'

She tugged at his arm but he pulled it free.

'We're already *there*!' he said inexplicably.

She stared at him.

'I don't know what you're saying,' she said at last.

He put up a warning finger.

'Listen!'

And this time she heard it, that high, childish voice, singing.

> *'Poor Mary sits a-weeping, a-weeping,*
>   *a-weeping,*
> *Poor Mary sits a-weeping on a bright*
>   *summer's day.'*

The song was as eerie in the vast ice-gold dawn as ever it had been under the moon, as unutterably lonely.

'She's here! In *your* time!'

'No! We're *there*!'

'But – it's daytime! You said yourself – she only ever comes at night!'

'Well, we ain't both dreaming!'

No, Minty thought, they were not. For some reason that strange child of the night was now here, if not in broad daylight, at least out of the shadows.

'At last! We'll see her!'

He nodded.

'Come on!'

Warily they stepped out and went stealthily, like hunters, in the direction of the voice. It was coming from somewhere beyond the moondial, she had strayed a long way from the house. Just as the song ended they saw her. She was sitting by the long lily pool, her back turned to them. She was cloaked as usual, in a soft grey blue, but with her hood pushed down. Her hair hung straight and fair.

As they tiptoed forward they heard her speaking softly.

'Daisy,' they heard her say. 'Day's Eye – that's what it says, in the book. You close at night, and open in the day. You and me are opposites, daisy. *I* curl up in the day and come out at night!'

Now they were nearly there, exchanging looks. What should they do, what say?

'You're my midsummer wish, daisy,' said the child gravely. 'To see you open up in the sun!'

They saw her hand lift the single daisy before her eyes.

'So it's midsummer day!' thought Minty.

The child shook her head, then scrambled to

her feet. She stood for a moment, then went slowly, almost fearfully, towards the edge of the pool. A few paces away, she stopped.

'Dare I . . .?' they heard her say. Then, 'No . . . I daren't . . . I must never look . . . never . . . But what if I shut my eyes, and then wash my face in the water? What if it'd be a kind of spell . . . for midsummer's day . . .?'

She took those few last paces to the water's edge. Then she dropped to her knees, leaned forward, and began to scoop up the water in her hands. The watchers saw the droplets flashing about her. Then, after only a few seconds, she straightened up and sat back on her heels, her face tilted up now, but still turned away from them.

'Let the sun dry it,' they heard her say. 'Oh, *please* let it work, please!'

She stayed like this a long time, and Minty guessed that her eyes were closed as she waited for the sun to dry their lids. Tom nudged her.

'Shall we—?' he whispered, and jerked his head towards the still figure. Minty frowned.

'No!'

Some kind of solemn ceremony was being performed by the child. They must wait. At last she suddenly gave her head a shake and slowly, hesitantly, put her hands up to her face.

'*Feels* the same . . .' they heard her say. 'Oh, but what if it isn't? But how can I tell? I daren't look down at my reflection, I daren't!'

Tom could contain himself no longer. He stepped forward.

'Sarah!' he said. 'Sarah?'

The child whirled round. Her hand flew up to her face. But not before Minty had glimpsed the dark, purple stain of a birthmark spreading over one cheek. She gasped. Now she understood.

'Oh Sarah!' she almost groaned with the pity she felt, and going forward she stretched out a hand to help her to her feet. But the girl, like some wild animal, had an instinct for flight. She was already on her feet and running, the long cloak streaming out behind her.

'Sarah! Stop! Please!'

'After her!' yelled Tom.

Minty saw the fugitive's head turn, saw the terror.

'No!' she cried, and pulled at his sleeve to stop him.

'Come *on*!' He wrenched his arm free and broke into a run.

'No!' Minty screamed. She caught up and grabbed him as he ran and felt the jacket tear.

'Now look what you've done! And if we don't get after her, we've lost her!'

'But she thinks we're like those others! She thinks we're after her!'

'Well, we are, ain't we!'

'No – I mean *really* after her!'

They stood looking at one another, gasping for breath.

'Did you – see?'

He nodded.

'Poor little devil!'

'Don't say that! Not – devil. It's what *they* said.'

She looked beyond him to see Sarah disappear

behind the large yews that marked the end of the path to the house.

'All right!' she said. 'Quick! She can't see us now.'

'Cut across here!' called Tom, veering off. 'We'll catch her up!'

'Keep behind the bushes! She mustn't see us!'

They ran without stopping until they reached the bottom of the seven shallow steps. From their hiding place behind the yew they saw that Sarah, halfway along the terrace, had stopped. Fearfully she was scanning the garden for her pursuers. Even from this distance Minty could see the livid mark on her cheek.

At last, evidently satisfied, Sarah turned again. She went trudging along the terrace, leaving the day behind, going back to prison.

They waited until she disappeared through the doorway to the courtyard, then made after her. They reached the stone passage just in time to see her entering the door Minty herself had gone through with Tom.

''Ere!' He sounded shocked. 'That's *my* door! What's she up to? Lady, she is – what's she doing going in there?'

They followed, running again. Once inside the house, with its maze of corridors, they could lose her. But there she was – they heard her first, those dragging footsteps. Then, hurrying, they saw her blue cloak, fair head. She pushed a huge panelled door and passed through, leaving it open behind her. They reached it and peered in just in time to see Sarah passing through yet another door on the far side of a room that was evidently part of the main house. There was heavy, gleaming furniture, walls lined with gilt-framed pictures, richly draped windows. Minty set off across it.

''Ere!' She turned. Tom was hanging back, his face all at once pinched and scared. 'Breakfast Room, this is! I ain't let in here! Skin me alive if they catch me in here!'

'They can't! It's *her* time, remember?'

They were through the second door now, and into an amazing crimson.

'Cor!' Tom was awestruck. 'Red Drawing Room, this is! Heard about it! Cor! Ain't it just red?'

It was. Carpet, walls, hangings smouldered, blazed. The very air breathed red.

Sarah had vanished. Minty crossed the room and came into a vast light entrance hall. There, on the great black and white diamonds of the floor, was that small blue figure, a chess piece.

At that moment there came other footsteps, a clatter and rattle. Sarah stopped in her tracks, Minty and Tom stiffened. A young woman appeared round a corner at the far side of the hall. She saw Sarah, her eyes stretched and she let out a shriek.

'Oh! Oh, Saints preserve me!'

Hastily she dropped one of the pails she was carrying, and with the free hand made the sign of the cross. She snatched up the pail again and hurried on, ran almost, past Sarah, past Tom and Minty, who stood dumbstuck by this proof of their invisibility.

'We *are* invisible!' breathed Tom.

'So we are,' thought Minty, 'even if he's only back a hundred years, and I'm two hundred. Equally invisible!'

Sarah turned slowly to gaze sadly after the maid who had crossed herself against her.

'It didn't work!' she whispered.

Then she saw Tom and Minty. Oddly, she seemed not to care. They stood locked, all three. Minty saw that tears were running down her cheeks, though she made no sign of weeping.

'Who are you?'

Minty stepped forward.

'We want to help you,' she said. 'We're friends.'

Sarah shook her head.

'I haven't got any,' she said. Then, 'What are friends?'

'I ain't got any, neither,' Tom said. 'Excepting *her*. Got a sister, but she ain't here. Dorrie. Eight, she is. That what you are?'

She nodded.

'Aren't you – afraid of me?'

'Of course not! Afraid?' Minty took a step forward, longing to reassure her.

'The others are. They call me devil's—'

'I know what they call you,' Minty said quickly. 'And you're not!'

'But I've got the devil's mark!'

'Sarah!'

The voice rang harshly, made all three jump. Minty saw the shadow of fear pass over Sarah's face.

'It's her!'

She turned and sped away.

'Here, Miss Vole! I'm coming!'

'Little devil! How dare you! What have I told you!'

Sarah had disappeared. Minty and Tom stood and listened. They heard sharp slaps, Sarah's cries, echoing in that cold stone hall.

They went after her, and reaching the foot of the stairs saw the pair turning the corner above them, Miss Vole dragging the child by the arm.

'Pig! Pig!' screamed Minty, and raced up after them. As she reached the first turn in the stairs she glimpsed them for an instant in a doorway to the left above her. Then came the slam of a door.

Tom and Minty reached the landing together, and stood panting. The door was open but there, within it, to the right, was another, smaller door – shut.

'Listen!' whispered Minty. She could hear the woman, Miss Vole, speaking quietly now.

'We're going in!'

Tom shrank back. He was breaking more rules than she. They were both breaking the law of time, but he was also breaking the law that said there were two worlds, and the line between them could never be crossed. He was a ragged kitchen boy who had already dared to cross that line, and was terrified of discovery.

'We're invisible! Tom! We must!'

His eyes were enormous, his thin arms wrapped about himself as if for protection.

'What if it was Dorrie in there!' she whispered urgently. 'She's only eight – same as Dorrie!'

He stared back, then nodded, though his teeth were chattering.

'As soon as the door's open, slip in after me, and I'll shut it,' she whispered. 'If she sees, just press up against the wall, here.'

He nodded again.

Minty took the huge brass knob and turned it gently. It made no sound, and nor did the door as she eased it open. Miss Vole was still speaking, very softly.

'I don't suppose, Sarah, you ever consider what my own life is like, shut up here, week in week out, with a monstrosity!'

They were inside the room. Minty closed the door, breath held. The room was large, and yellow in the same way as the Red Drawing Room was red. The floor, the drapes of the huge four-poster bed, the floor-length curtains, all were yellow as sunlight. The tall black shape that was Miss Vole stood, back turned, between themselves and the light. Sarah was blocked from their view by the woman towering over her.

'They don't pay me very much, you know,' the soft voice continued. 'I shall never be rich, waiting after you. And no one speaks to me, unless they can help it. Do you know why, Sarah . . .? Because they are afraid of me. Because they believe that something evil must rub off on me, being with you . . . day in, day out. They may be right. Perhaps it does. Who knows . . .?'

Sarah made no reply, though they could hear her convulsive sobs.

'I sometimes wonder whether I exist at all . . .' the voice continued. 'I sometimes wonder whether I shall go mad . . .'

There was a silence. Then the dark shape gave a sudden shudder.

'Shut in here!' the voice spat. 'Why do you never look at me? *Look* at me!'

Then, with a swift movement, she stepped towards the windows, past Sarah.

'There!' cried Miss Vole, and with a single sweep pulled down a yellow drape. It fell heavily to the floor, revealing a long, gilt-framed mirror.

'Don't turn round!' she hissed. ''Ware the glass!'

Sarah screamed and buried her face in both hands.

Minty, too, let out a gasp. The face she saw reflected in the mirror – long and white and narrow-lipped – was that of Miss Raven! Her instinct was to turn, run. Surely this woman, whom she recognized, despite the strange costume and swept-back hair, must see and recognize herself? But she showed no sign of even sensing the presence of the two strangers, cowering by the door.

Miss Vole stood before the glass, eyes glittering, turning a little this way and that, surveying herself from head to foot.

'I am still here,' she announced. 'At least the mirror tells me that! August Vole, thirty-seven years old, spinster, penniless, a servant!'

She gazed deeply into her own eyes, drew herself up.

'But I am a beautiful woman – such a beautiful white skin!' She put up her hands to touch her own unblemished sallow cheeks. 'Do you not think me beautiful, Sarah?'

Sarah, her face still buried, made a choking sound. Miss Vole spun from the mirror, seized her by the shoulders and shook her.

'Do you?' she spat. 'Answer me! Do you?'

'Oh yes – yes!'

'And beautiful faces need mirrors, Sarah.' Now the voice was soft again. 'So today I shall spend with my own reflection!'

She gave the child a sudden push, and Sarah stumbled and caught one of the bedposts to steady herself.

'Better bury your head, dear,' said Miss Vole. 'The mirrors are coming out to play!'

As they watched, horrorstruck, Sarah clambered frantically on to the high bed, scrabbling at the heavy covers, and buried herself there, pulling her cloak about her.

Miss Vole watched her with a thin smile. She turned and tugged at another drape, unveiled another mirror.

'There!'

She advanced towards the fireplace, and the heavy swathes that hung above it.

'What a difference it makes to the room!' she said, as light flashed from a wide, triple glass. 'I feel better already! I wish that you could see it.'

She turned mockingly and surveyed the crumpled heap on the bed.

'But you can't, of course. Poor Sarah. If ever *you* look into a mirror, we know what will happen, don't we?'

A muffled choking sound from the folds of the grey-blue cloak.

'Tell me, Sarah, what would happen. What would happen first?'

There was a long pause.

'The – glass would – crack!' Sarah's voice was hardly audible.

'I don't hear you! Louder, please! Again – what would happen first?'

'The – the glass would – crack!'

The woman laughed.

'That's better. Yes. The glass would crack. And then . . . and then, Sarah . . .?'

'Oh no, please!' The child was sobbing again. 'The – the devil – w-would—' the voice broke off.

Minty, her heart painfully clenched with pity, could hardly bear it.

'The devil would get you!' hissed that terrible voice.

And then, it seemed, Tom could bear it no longer. He wrenched open the door and was gone. Minty hesitated long enough to see Miss Vole, startled, turn and stare at the open door.

'Who is it? Who's there?'

'Her turn to be afraid!' thought Minty, and went after Tom.

Down the wide staircase she raced. She turned the corner into the chessboard hall and saw him stop dead in his tracks, almost in headlong collision with a mincing footman in powdered wig, bearing a silver tray.

'Blimey! No! Help!' He dodged and sped on, Minty in pursuit.

She caught up with him in the Red Drawing Room. He was leaning against a heavy plush chair, bent almost double, coughing, fighting for breath.

'Why – did – you run?' gasped Minty. 'We should've stopped! Helped her!'

He lifted his head, his eyes streaming, powerless to speak as paroxysms of coughing shook his thin shoulders.

'Daresn't!' he managed at last. The fit had passed. 'You – 'eard what she said! The devil!'

Minty stared at him aghast. Surely, surely he did not believe it? That little Sarah, with her sweet, marked face, was really the devil's child? As she stared she saw a thin scarlet line running from the corner of his mouth.

He must have felt it. He spat, lifted his arm and wiped his mouth with the back of his hand. He looked down. They both saw the smeared blood on the white skin.

'Oh Tom!' whispered Minty.

He looked at her, his face suddenly hard and old.

'That does it! I'm finished! With her – and you! You hear me! I ain't playing these devil's games no more! I'm going to be six foot tall and a footman, I'm going to fetch our Dorrie here and—'

His voice dwindled to a pale echo and faded. His thin shape dissolved into the mist of redness.

'Tom! Please – oh Tom – no!'

He had gone, deliberately left her alone in this alien time. It was useless to call him. He could never come against his will.

She went back slowly the way she had come, through the rich, oppressive rooms, up the chill stone steps and into the open air. Half dazed, she was aware that the courtyard was thronged with people, horses.

'They don't see me,' she thought. 'I'm not even a fly on the wall. I'm a daylight ghost.'

As she turned and went back into the garden, along that wide terrace, she felt as if she were indeed a daylight ghost, faint and powerless. Even her thoughts were faded and unreal, passing in wisps. Why had Tom vanished? She knew why. He had gone because he wanted to go, because he was frightened, because he saw his own dreams lean and topple . . . because he believed in Miss Vole's devil.

She lifted her chin.

'But I don't!' she said fiercely, out loud.

She saw that she was level with those sneering masks, so cunningly concealed among the harmless fruit and flowers. She looked at them, first to left, then to right.

'Your eyes remind me of hers!' she said. 'Evil and hateful!'

And as she spoke her ears were filled with whispers, and she caught snatches of Miss Vole's soft, insistent voice.

'I sometimes wonder whether I shall go mad . . .

better bury your head, dear, the mirrors are coming out to play!'

Minty screamed. She put her hands over her ears and ran blindly towards the moondial, towards safety. And as she ran, the spiteful, chattering voices pursued her.

'Poor Sarah ... If ever *you* look into a mirror, we know what will happen, don't we ...?'

She had reached the moondial.

'The glass will crack ... the glass will crack ... the glass will crack!'

Minty took her hands from her ears and clasped the head of the winged boy.

'I want to go home!' she sobbed. 'Please! Please!'

SEVEN

'Tom won't come to me,' Minty thought. 'He's frightened. I must go to him.'

She, too, was afraid, remembering that terrible racking cough, the blood.

'But he must help me. I can't do it alone.'

The pattern she was looking for had started to make itself that morning. She, Tom and Sarah had actually stood for an instant like frozen chesspieces on the chequered floor. The game had been set in motion.

She looked about the graveyard where she was sitting, alone because the cats had dissolved with the dew. Then she sighed and rose because she had to go back to the cottage, breakfast and Miss Raven who was Miss Vole. She shivered at the thought of the enemy within the house.

'But at least she can't make me a prisoner, like poor Sarah.'

She tried to recall that yellow room with its creamy drapes and shining mirrors. It had been quite bare apart from the bed and perhaps a chair or two. She tried to imagine Sarah's life, with the bareness, the silence and the long hours. The room had been at the front of the house, where the view went on forever over the wide park and hills beyond. Sarah must number the time by the way the light slanted through the long windows. For her, time must be a tortoise.

Her eye fell on the yews that lined the path and she thought that they were the tortoises among trees, and perhaps that was why they were planted in churchyards, where time had ceased to matter.

Before leaving she went to the corner by the tower and into the secret weather that was always there, into the little icy gusts. They had been there right from the very beginning, the first sign and still she did not know the reason. Her eye fell on the tiny thumbnail headstone: E. L. 1871, and she wondered fleetingly if that was a clue. She could not think why.

At the cottage Aunt Mary and Miss Raven had already started breakfast. They looked up as she entered and she composed her face and tried not to think of Miss Vole.

'So *there* you are!' exclaimed Aunt Mary.

'Am I late?' Minty asked. 'Sorry. I lost count of the time.'

'I'm not talking about late, Minty,' Aunt Mary said. She put down her cup. Her cheeks were pink.

'I do not expect to come down in the morning and find my front door open!'

'But it wasn't! I closed it – I know I did!'

'Unlocked. You can't imagine what a shock! And then when I found you gone . . .'

'You might have been out all night,' put in Miss Raven. She paused. 'You weren't, I suppose?'

'Of course not! I just got up early, that's all.'

'And fetched your aunt's key from its hiding place,' Miss Raven observed. 'That was a sly trick.'

'I won't have it!' Aunt Mary's voice was trembling at the thought of dawn burglars creeping through her neat house with dew on their boots, stealing every stick of furniture in the place.

'I'm sorry,' said Minty again. 'I'm *sorry*, Aunt Mary. I didn't think.'

'That, of course, is the trouble with children,' said Miss Raven. 'They don't think.'

'Next time I'll lock the door behind me,' Minty said.

'Oh no,' said Miss Raven. 'Your aunt will put the key somewhere else, somewhere safe.'

Minty was horrorstruck. She had to go out again at night, she knew it. Now she was to be made a prisoner of the night just as Sarah was a prisoner of the day. When would they ever meet?

'While you are staying in my house I am responsible for you,' said Aunt Mary. 'I must know where you are. I can't have you running off on your own at all hours of the day.'

'And night,' supplied Miss Raven.

'And night,' repeated Aunt Mary mechanically, though fortunately she did not seem to take this idea seriously.

'I may have to go out at night myself, Mrs Bowyer,' Miss Raven said. 'In the course of my work. That, of course, is a different matter.'

'Quite a different matter, Miss Raven.'

Minty sat there, trapped and panicking. She was to be shut in at night, Miss Raven let out. As soon as possible she made her escape up to her room. To relieve her feelings she put on another tape and began to tell Kate her latest adventures. By now she was used to it, felt that she was actually talking to her mother – even found herself asking her questions, as if she were really there.

When she came down Miss Raven had gone out – to the House, Aunt Mary said, to investigate.

'As if she didn't already know!' Minty thought. Aloud, she said, 'Is it all right if I go out now? I thought I'd go over and see if there were any children about.'

'That's a good idea!' said Aunt Mary, who could not know what kind of children Minty meant. 'That's what you need – some company of your own age. Haven't you found some friends in the village?'

'Well – sort of,' Minty told her.

She was really going to see World, but decided to go the long way round, through the garden. When she reached the moondial she paused. It was impossible to pass it by without a glance or a word. She looked at the two stone faces, remote and inscrutable.

'You mean something,' she told them. 'I know you do. And I'm going to find out what.'

Then she left them, and wandered towards the House, not along the usual path but to the right, where she had never properly explored. In front of the orangery was a large circular pool and she saw, as she had seen yesterday on her tour with Miss Raven, that it was empty.

'Do they ever fill it?' she wondered, and hoped so. An empty pool was a waste of reflections.

A wall ran along the edge of the garden and Minty saw a curious, curved recess. It was of pinkish terracotta, and spaced round it in niches were five small carved basins. Above them, in the centre, was an odd, leonine head, neither man nor beast.

'Basins, but not taps!' She was puzzled. 'What are they for?'

She gazed into the hollow eyes of the mask but they seemed to be looking beyond her, over the dry, unreflecting pool. Bees hummed and nuzzled among the warm stone garlands and the pale ivy. It was a mystery.

Minty shrugged. Perhaps she was trying to read a meaning where there was none. Perhaps it was all just a pretty fancy.

As she approached the House she went cautiously, alert for any sign of the Raven, as she now thought of her. Black. Bird of ill omen. It was with relief that she turned the corner into the drive and saw World there by his lodge.

'Morning,' he greeted her. 'Getting the sun into my old bones.'

'World . . .' she began. Then, 'Do you mind if I call you World? It doesn't sound right, *Mr* World.'

'You call me that,' he told her. 'It's who I am. Old World . . . they all call me that.'

'World ... I wanted to ask you ... do you know anything about that moo— sundial?'

'In the garden yon?' He jerked his head.

'Yes. The one on the yew path.'

'Can't say I do, a deal. Interested in it, are you?'

'Yes. I want to find out who they are – the man and the boy.'

'Tell you what I *have* got,' he said. 'I've got a book. Had it since I was a little lad – hours I'd spend puzzling over it. All about sundials, it is.'

'Oh yes, I'd like that. I don't know anything about them, really.'

'I'll fetch it.'

He disappeared into the shadows. He returned carrying an old book with a stone sundial festooned in roses on the cover, and gave it to her.

'You'll learn a lot from that. I did. The queerest things. They've stuck in my mind all these years.'

'What kind of things?'

He ticked them off on his fingers.

'Well, for instance ... clock time is mean time. Sundial time is what they call apparent time.

225

And you know what the only *real* time is, exact time?'

'What?'

'Startime!'

He sounded triumphant, as if the fact confirmed something that he already knew in his bones.

'Startime!' Minty felt a long, delicious shiver. 'You mean – moontime!'

'Moontime! Well, ain't heard of that one. But moon and stars are out together . . . I don't know . . . I don't know.'

'Ah, but I do,' thought Minty. Then, out loud, 'The only real time!'

'That's what it says. You read it.'

'Oh, I will. And thank you!'

'And – about that sundial. I'll ask one or two folk. Find out for you.'

'Oh, would you? Oh, thank you, World – oh, I do love you!'

She wanted to throw her arms around him but could not, partly because of the book she was hugging and partly because she was shy, but she smiled at him and he smiled back and she felt herself warmed.

Then the smile went and his face was suddenly shadowed.

'Those children . . .' he said. 'They're in trouble.'

'I know.'

'It's as if they're getting nearer . . . crying . . . it breaks my heart to hear 'em . . .'

'I know,' she said again. 'But not for much longer. I promise.'

She made the promise with utter certainty. She did not know how she would rescue Tom and Sarah, loose them to run free forever in moontime, but she would.

World was smiling again.

'You're a good 'un!' he told her. 'Knew you was, minute I set eyes on you.'

'And you,' she said. 'You're a good 'un!' and she laughed.

She liked the expression, she'd use it to Kate. 'You're a good 'un, Mum!' she'd say, and watch for the reaction.

'What about that mother of yours, then?' It was as if he had read her thoughts.

'Oh, she's getting better, thank you,' said Minty steadily. 'Invisibly.'

'That's the way. Good. I'm glad. Here's customers. You get off and read that book.'

Minty left him, not for the cottage that was not home, but to find a quiet place to lie and read. She made towards the front of the House. There she stopped on the wide lawns, looking up to see if she could make out which was the Yellow Room she had visited.

'I'm outside now, so what was left indoors will be on the right,' she worked out. Her gaze travelled across the upper storey and came to rest on two long windows at the extreme right.

'That one,' she decided, and as she gazed a figure appeared and stood as if looking out. At this distance the face was only a pale blur, but Minty had a sudden swift conviction that it was a face she knew, white and narrow, with hooded eyes.

'The Raven!' she gasped. 'Or – her!'

She turned and moved swiftly away, not running, because that might give her away, simply trying to escape as quickly as possible from those watching eyes. She could feel them on her back, following her.

Once out of view of the house she saw ahead of her the long pool where Sarah had bathed her face, hoping for a midsummer magic that would wash away that dark, disfiguring stain. At the edge of the water she stood gazing down at her own reflection.

'Has she really never seen herself ...?' she wondered? 'But she's got a lovely face. And – she thinks she's some kind of monster!'

There was a boy in her street who used to have a birthmark on his face. Now it had vanished, by the magic not of a midsummer pool but of a laser. Times had changed. Yet time was still the same. It was a mystery.

'Tom, too,' she thought. 'All those children, dying of consumption, and nowadays not one does. And Mum ... If we'd been living in those times ...'

She dared not complete the thought. No breathing, sighing machines, no busy screens, no tape recorders for the telling of a story that made the very idea of time a riddle.

Turning from the pool she threw herself down on the grass and opened the book. She turned the pages, thinking of World turning them all those years ago when he was a child. Soon she was absorbed. There was a whole chapter about the inscriptions that are found on sundials. Most of the ones she had ever seen were modern ones, and simply said 'Sunny Hours'. These were much better.

'For the Night Cometh – cutting off all Power of Passing of Time.'

That fitted, she thought. That was just it. Night-time did not pass, it became moontime, which had nothing to do with clocks. There was a Latin motto: *Lux et Umbra Vicissim, sed semper Amor.* Beneath it was the translation: Light and Shadow by turns, but always Love.

'I like that,' she thought, and memorized it to repeat to Kate.

She read on. Everything World had told her was true. Star, or sidereal, time *was* the only exact time. She glanced at her watch.

'So much for you!' she told it.

All the same she kept an eye on it. If she were late for dinner as well as breakfast, she might be stopped from going off on her own altogether.

'Mr Benson telephoned,' Aunt Mary told her when she got back. 'He says he'll come for you at two o'clock.'

'Mum! Oh – has she woken up?'

'He didn't say. Said something about seeing for yourself.'

'Oh! Those monitor things, he means. Oh – she must've! Oh Aunt Mary!'

She threw her arms about her, but Aunt Mary did not seem comfortable, and merely patted her back awkwardly in response.

'Now don't go getting too excited, dear. We don't know yet. You don't want to be disappointed.'

She extricated herself and turned away to the sink.

'Dinner in ten minutes!'

When Minty heard Mr Benson draw up she pushed the cassette into her pocket and ran.

'See you later!' she called.

Mr Benson was standing there waiting, and he opened his arms and she ran into them. He lifted her and swung her round.

'Hurray!' she cried.

He set her down and they stood looking at one another.

'Is she really . . .?'

'You want me to tell you? Or d'you want to see for yourself?'

'Oh . . . see for myself, I suppose! But hurry!'

This time when Minty went through the hospital doors she did not even notice the smell. The corridors seemed as long as ever, though. The journey to the room where Kate lay seemed endless. Then, when at last she reached it, she inexplicably hesitated. Part of her did not want to go in – dared not. She drew a deep breath.

In the room everything at first seemed the same.

Those screens with their flickering green curves – were they the same? She could not tell. She looked towards the bed, at Kate herself. Something was different! The tubes had gone! Her mother lay pale and sleeping as before, but not with that awful, unnatural stillness.

'Minty?'

She turned. The nurse was smiling at her and she too was human now, without the mask.

'Say hello to her,' she said. 'I'll be back in a minute,' and she was gone, leaving the two of them together.

Slowly Minty advanced. She saw on the locker the familiar headset, in it her own cassette with its telling of another world, of moontime. She looked down at her mother for a moment, then touched her arm.

'Mum, it's me, Minty!'

Did she only imagine that now the lips were moving?

'Have you been listening to my story ... about Tom and Sarah, and the moondial? There's lots more to tell you. I went again, this morning, and—'

She stopped. Slightly, ever so slightly, Kate's eyelids were fluttering. Her head was turning ... and then she was looking straight into Minty's own eyes.

'Minty ...' she whispered. 'Minty!'

Then the tears came, she could not help them. Dropping to her knees by the bed Minty buried her face and felt the familiar warmth of her mother's body.

'Oh Mum ... Mum ... you've come back!'

'*Was* it my story that brought her back?' Minty asked.

They were driving back to Belton. Kate had not spoken again during the visit, but it did not matter. She was on the way back from wherever it was she had been, and would come a little further each day, the doctor had told her.

'I'm sure it was,' Mr Benson said. 'It must be some story!'

'It is,' she said simply, and that was all. It was not a story for telling in the ordinary way.

'Partly that,' he continued, 'and partly your voice, telling it. I've known quite a few cases like this. There was one little kid they played tapes to of all his mates in his class, over and over again, hundreds of times. Then one day he just opened his eyes and said, 'You lot are bonkers! Why don't you say something different for a change?'

They both laughed.

'You could say it's the same in every case, though, where it works,' he said. 'It's caring enough that brings people back. Even when it's just music. That's the common denominator.'

She glanced sideways at him.

'You're a good 'un, Mr Benson!' she told him.

He looked back at her, surprised, pleased.

'John?' he suggested.

'All right –John,' she agreed.

'Well, that *is* lovely news!' said Aunt Mary when she was told. 'Did she have much to say?'

'No, just my name.'

'Oh well, never mind. It's a start.'

'It sounds as if there's a long way to go yet,' observed Miss Raven. Minty regarded them both with cold eyes.

'I'll give you some roses out of the garden to take next time you go,' Aunt Mary said. 'They'll do her heart good. That looks an interesting book you've got in your room, Minty.'

'What book?' She wished her room could be private, as it was at home. Everyone should have a place of their own, quite private, Kate said.

'That one about sundials.'

Minty stiffened. She glanced at Miss Raven and met her eyes, hard and inquisitive.

'Where did you get hold of it?' Aunt Mary was asking. 'It looks very old.'

'I – borrowed it.' She did not mention World. 'I was bored, so I borrowed it. Not very interesting, really.'

'Might *I* borrow it, Araminta?' said Miss Raven. 'There's a very interesting sundial in the formal gardens, Mrs Bowyer, depicting two winged figures. Eros and Chronos, I'm told.'

She knew their names! She had already found out what Minty herself was longing to know. What had she said they were? She had spoken the names so quickly and unexpectedly that Minty had missed them – and she dared not ask.

'I haven't finished it yet,' she said. 'Might as well finish it, now I've started. Might come in useful at school.'

'I thought it looked very educational,' said Aunt Mary approvingly. 'So many children these days waste their time reading rubbish.'

'Much,' thought Minty, '*you* know about it!'

She went out, not because she had anywhere to go, but to escape their presence.

'I do not feel we have anything to say to one another,' she told herself, quoting one of Kate's sayings about people she didn't much care for.

In any case she wanted to hug to herself the joy that had been welling up in her since that moment in the hospital when Kate had lifted her drowsy lids and whispered her name. Now that she knew her mother was going to be all right she could admit the terrible dread that had been haunting her – that she might die.

There was no one about in the churchyard and so Minty, needing something to do, on the spur of the moment decided on an experiment.

'I'll go and *sit* in that windy patch,' she thought. 'It's got to have a meaning. I might find out if I sit and wait.'

She sat on the coarse, yellowing grass just off the path. If she tilted her head right back she could just glimpse one of the gilt pennants on the tower, glinting and motionless. The cold wind blew about her, lifting her hair, cooling her cheeks, and she marvelled that no one else ever seemed to notice.

Then she began to feel another kind of chill, one that lifted the hairs at the nape of her neck. The skin on her arms broke out in goose pimples.

'Someone walking on my grave,' she thought, 'or – something!'

'Minty! Minty!' came a hoarse whisper.

Turning her head she saw, incredibly, Tom, standing only a few yards away, just inside the iron gates. But this was a strange Tom with burning eyes, his face white and stricken.

'Tom!' She jumped up and went to him because he seemed frozen there, as if he would never move. He stared at her without speaking.

'Come on, Tom,' she said gently. 'Over here.'

They were standing directly in the path from churchyard to gardens, they could be disturbed at any moment. She took his arm and led him unprotestingly into the quiet graveyard on the far side of the church. There she let go his arm and as she did so he dropped to the ground, face down. He lay there, racked with inconsolable sobs that had been buried, she guessed, for weeks, months, under his jaunty manner and fine talk of being a footman.

She waited a while, then dropped to her knees beside him. She touched his shoulder.

'Tom. What is it? Tell me. Please.'

After a long time and without raising his head he choked out a single word.

'Dorrie!'

'Oh no!' His little sister, Dorrie, who was living

with old Ma Barker and gutter-picking in London. Dorrie, who was such a card, and for whose sake he was trying to stretch himself to six feet tall – something had happened to her.

'What about her?' Minty's own voice was trembling.

'She's spitting!' Still he did not raise his head but all at once, the words out, he went limp, just lay there, the shudders subsiding.

Spitting? What ...? Then she had a picture of Tom himself, in the Red Drawing Room, of the racking cough, the thin line of blood ... and she understood.

'Oh – Tom!'

There seemed no words of comfort. The helplessness she felt was followed by an upsurge of rage at the cruelty and unfairness of it all. Tom – already an orphan, Tom, bravely setting out from London to seek his fortune at Belton, where he was cuffed and beaten, with never a kind word. Her own eyes were blinded with tears.

'Done now!' she heard him say. Brushing an arm

across her eyes, she saw him struggle up, wiping his own face on his jacket sleeve, fighting back to his everyday self. 'Ain't no sense blubbing. Waste o' water!'

She smiled despite herself.

'Our Dorrie don't cry. Know what she does? Screeches! Cor, if you could hear 'er! Hear 'er in Stepney, if wind's blowing the right way! Screech?'

He shook his head, as if the words did not exist that would describe Dome's screeching.

'It's what I feel like doing,' Minty said. 'Screeching.'

He looked at her now.

'Didn't run off 'cos I was frit, you know!' he said. 'Don't you think it!'

'I know,' said Minty.

'I ain't never frit!' he said. 'Not of nuffin!'

'I know,' she said again.

'Got to get her out,' he went on. 'Sarah. Ain't we?'

'We've got to get her out,' Minty told him, 'and we've got to get you out.'

'Me? Where? How'll *I* get out?'

'I don't know, yet,' she admitted. 'Not exactly. But we will.'

'Something to do with that old sundial, I reckon.'

'Moondial. Yes. Into moontime . . .'

'Moontime?'

She nodded.

'No Maggs, no Ma Crump, no beatings.'

'You mean – never go back? Ever?' He sounded fearful.

'Tonight,' she heard herself say. She had not known it for certain until this minute, but now she was sure. It was something to do with things coming full circle, with Kate having opened her eyes again. The game was drawing to a close. They had all been caught up in it together – Kate, herself, Tom, Sarah – and now it would be resolved.

She was all at once aware of the coarse grass pricking her palm, the croon of pigeons in the high trees, the hot dry scent of yew, the nowness of the moment. She saw Tom, who was her friend and yet a kitchen boy from Victorian times, under the full wide light of a twentieth-century sun, and knew that if this moment were real, all things were possible.

She studied him, noting detail – the grime of his smudged face, the shock of unkempt hair, the missing buttons, even the holes in his clumsy boots. He was real.

''Ere! What you staring at?'

'Sorry. Just making sure you're real.'

'Cheek! Don't you start that up again! You ain't half rum. Rummest girl I've know – 'cept Dorrie, o' course.'

'Good!' She was elated by the compliment. The idea of being rum appealed to her. 'We're both real. And her – Sarah.'

He jumped to his feet.

'And pigs can fly and the moon's made of green cheese and I'll be six foot high yet or my name ain't Teddy Larkin!'

He was doing his stretching now, arms poking a foot out of his ragged cuffs, white shins gleaming above his boots.

'What? What did you say?'

She scrambled up and tugged at his sleeve.

'What?' He didn't stop.

'*What* did you say your name was?'

He lowered his arms.

'Teddy Larkin, o' course!'

'But – you said it was Tom! Tom short for Edward, you said!'

'S'right. So it is. Same as yours is Minty short for Penelope.'

'But – that was a joke! I thought you were joking.'

'Look,' he said patiently, 'I'm Teddy Larkin, right? But kitchen boys here is always called Tom. See?'

She didn't.

'What – you mean *all* kitchen boys?'

'S'right. Got to be. Someone yells "Tom!" and it means kitchen boys. And we all come running. See?'

'You're really all called Tom?'

'Course. Can't expect old Crump and the nobs to go learning all our names off.'

'But – don't you mind?' It seemed to Minty that not to be allowed your own name, to be carelessly called

'Tom' as in 'Tom, Dick or Harry' was terrible. You and your name were one and the same thing, almost.

He shrugged.

'You gets used to it. There's three of us 'ere, all Toms. Or Whatsyername. Get called that an' all – Whatsyername.'

'I think I'll have to go on calling you Tom,' said Minty slowly. 'Because that's who you are now, to me. D'you mind?'

'Course not. Why should I?'

'But to me you're a proper Tom – not just a kitchen one.'

He nodded, and began his stretching and snuffing again. Then the coughing started.

'Tom!'

He looked at her inquiringly.

'Tonight!'

He was still wheezing and fighting for breath.

'We'll meet by the moondial. Midnight. Will you do it?'

'I'll try. Don't always work, though, do it? Times I've tried and it ain't worked.'

'But it's working better, all the time. Haven't you noticed? It's as if – if you really need it to, it will!'

'Like just now,' he said slowly. 'I came looking for you. Had to tell you. About Dorrie.'

She felt hugely and absurdly honoured.

'You needed me,' she said. 'Like I needed you that first time we met.'

They stared at one another.

'And Sarah – she needs us both,' Tom said.

It was as simple as that, really, Minty thought. There was nothing complicated about moontime. It was the most natural thing in the world.

'Midnight, then,' she said. 'On the stroke.'

'Well . . .' He hesitated. 'Near nuff, anyhow.'

'Aren't there any clocks where you are?'

'Clocks, all right. Great ticking things and bing bong bang morning noon and night!'

She guessed then.

'But you can't tell the time.'

'Know when it's time to get up,' he said defensively. 'Know when it's time to kip. And belly tells me when it's time for dinner. Don't need no clocks for that.'

'Look – see this?' She held out her wrist.

He peered disbelievingly.

'A little 'un! A little arm clock!'

'That's right. And look, see those little fingers?'

'One of 'em's bigger,' he said.

'Yes. And when the little one ... no. I'll tell you what.'

She unfastened the watch and held it out.

'Here – you put it on!'

'Me?'

'Hold your wrist out. I'll put it on for you.'

Obediently he stuck out his arm. She felt as she did tying a young child's shoelaces. With a pang she noticed again how thin his wrist and hand were, the bones fragile and just beneath the skin, like those of a young bird. She fastened the buckle.

'There!'

He could not take his eyes off it. He moved his arm, first one way then another, posing it, admiring. He was enchanted. Unable to contain himself, he began to prance about, as if he had entirely forgotten her.

'An arm clock, I've got an arm clock!'

'No one's ever given him anything before!' thought Minty, and knew that although she had meant only to lend it, she would never ask for it back.

'Now I'll show you what to do.' It was easiest, she decided, to show him half past eleven, the fingers making an almost straight line.

'When the big finger's at the bottom, here, and the little finger there, right at the top, then it's time to set out,' she told him.

'There – and there!' He pointed.

'That's it.'

'Best put it in my pocket,' he said. 'If old Ma Crump sees it she'll have it off me, and me backside black and blue!'

He unfastened the strap, took a last, delighted look at his prize, and put it in his pocket.

'We don't *know* it'll work,' he said. 'Us both being there at the same time. Not for sure.'

'No,' she agreed, 'we don't.'

From the corner of her eye she glimpsed a flash of ginger. Turning, she saw that same solitary cat that had come so astonishingly to Miss Raven's call. It regarded her now with unwinking amber stare. It seemed to be watching, listening even – a spy.

'Puss!' she called. 'Puss!'

The cat did not move.

''Orrible-looking object!' And Tom, before she could stop him, had stooped, picked up a stone and thrown it. There was a chink as it struck the gravestone and then the cat was gone.

'Oh – you shouldn't have!'

She was filled with a superstitious dread. For a moment she stared at the space where the cat had been, then whirled round.

'Tom!'

He too had vanished, as if he had thrown the stone into time itself and set up widening rings that had drawn him into them, like a whirlpool.

'You shouldn't have done it!' she repeated, and looked about the churchyard for a sign of the cat. There was none.

'Gone to find the Raven?' she wondered, and shivered.

Then, with a shock, she saw World. She had become so used to seeing him at his post in the lodge that she had not imagined him in any other setting. His figure, bent over a grave, seemed incongruous, at once familiar and unfamiliar. She approached.

'Hello, World.'

'Why – you, is it?' He straightened, though he was still bowed, the sunlight flooding his ancient face.

'Just paying my respects.' He gestured towards the flowers. He looked at her keenly.

'Look as if you've seen a ghost,' he observed.

'I have.' The words were on her lips but she did not speak them. She was used to keeping secrets. Besides, she could not think of Tom as a ghost. She had touched him, felt his warm breath and knew his story.

'Got something for you.' World was rummaging in his pockets now and withdrew a scrap of paper. 'Got them names for you. The sundial. Wrote 'em down – bit out of the common, see. Chronos and Eros. Greek, they are.'

He handed her the paper and Minty stared down at the two strange names. She recognized them as being the ones the Raven had said. She was unaccountably let down, deflated. They meant nothing to her.

'Oh, thank you, World.'

'Them's their proper names,' he told her. 'But they've got meanings in English.'

'Meanings?' She snatched at the word.

'Aye. Chronos – that's Time.'

'Time!'

'And Eros, that's Love.'

The small winged boy, of course – Cupid – he stood for Love. She might have known it.

EIGHT

'I shall take the key with me!' Miss Raven was saying. 'That will be the safest thing.'

'Oh, there you are, Minty,' said Aunt Mary. 'Miss Raven is going on a ghost hunt tonight!'

'And I shall wear my special ghost-hunting outfit,' Miss Raven informed them. 'I'll fetch it for you to see.'

She went out.

'She really is rather strange,' Aunt Mary whispered. 'Can she really see ghosts, do you think?'

'I shouldn't be surprised,' said Minty. 'I think she's a witch.'

'Oh Minty!'

Minty had a swift memory of the scene in the graveyard – the chink of stone on stone, then the orange cat shooting among the tombs. It had been spying. It had already told its mistress of the midnight assignation. Why else should Miss Raven have decided to go on her ghost hunt tonight?

'There!'

Miss Raven appeared in the doorway and Minty, looking up, had a distinct, physical shock. For an instant she saw, impossible among her aunt's bric à brac and chintzes – a witch!

A swirling black cloak enveloped the woman and she spread out her arms and postured like some great bird of omen. The Raven.

'Well?' she cried. She was almost twitching with excitement.

'Very – nice,' ventured Aunt Mary.

'It has a hood, too!' She pulled it up, and Minty was reminded of another hood, another face.

'There! The perfect disguise!'

'Shouldn't it be white?' asked Minty coldly.

'White? Whatever do you mean?'

'For a ghost. Aren't they usually supposed to be white?'

'I'm not trying to look like a ghost, silly girl!'

'Oh,' said Minty. 'Sorry. I thought you were.'

'Think!' said Miss Raven exultantly. 'I am anonymous! I might be from any age, in such a costume. Ghosts are sensitive, you see, and easily frightened. If one were to appear and to see me, then it would simply assume that I am from its own time. Now do you see?'

'What a sensible idea, Miss Raven,' said Aunt Mary limply.

Minty herself said nothing. She could hardly discount the theory as crackpot. She had herself worn a long nightdress and duffel in order not to alarm Sarah. It occurred to her that Miss Raven's black cloak would blend secretly with the night, would make her only a moving shadow, all but invisible.

It was too late now for Minty to change the time of her meeting with Tom. The die was cast. She had an inexplicable feeling of calmness, lightness, even. What was going to happen tonight was inevitable, beyond her control. All she had to do was play her part.

Even as she stood there she coolly decided which window she would use as an exit into the garden.

'The steward was very helpful about my going into the House,' Miss Raven was saying. 'I shall be free to go wherever I please. I have definite feelings about some of the rooms.'

'Make sure you don't look in a mirror!' With a shock Minty heard her own voice say the words. She did not even think them, they seemed to say themselves.

'What?' Miss Raven's voice was sharp. 'What did you say?'

'It's – just something I heard,' Minty said. 'That if you see a ghost in a mirror, then ... then ...' She paused. She looked Miss Raven straight in the eye. 'The devil gets you!'

'Minty!' She heard her aunt's shocked voice.

'I – I—!' gasped Miss Raven. 'I – never heard of such a thing! Oh! I—'

She swept her cloak about her and was gone.

'Minty! Whatever made you say such a thing!'

'I don't know,' said Minty, which was true. 'I'm sorry' – which was not.

'Frightening her like that!'

'She did seem rather frightened,' Minty agreed. 'I wonder why? I mean, she's not very scared of ghosts, is she?'

'Oh – I'll be glad when she's gone!'

Minty was surprised. Perhaps Aunt Mary, too, sensed something, was made uneasy.

'And so shall I!' said Minty, and the pair smiled at one another, united by their admission. 'When *will* she go?'

'Oh, at any time. She said she never stayed anywhere long. She said . . . now, what was it? Oh yes – she came and went as the spirit moved her!'

Later, in her room, Minty made her preparations. First, she told Kate about Tom's appearance in the graveyard that morning, and about Dorrie.

'And it's going to be tonight, Mum!' she told her. 'I don't know what's going to happen, I can't even imagine – but something! I know it in my bones.' She paused. 'And Mum . . . I think I'm going to a dangerous place tonight . . .'

256

She hesitated, switched off the microphone, and nodded slowly.

'Not even sure that I shall come back . . .'

When the night's work was done, perhaps she herself would have stepped out of time for good and all, would run forever in moontime.

'And never grow up,' she thought. 'Stay a child, forever and ever . . . strange . . .'

She removed the cassette, wrote on the label, and put it in an envelope addressed to Mr Benson. Then she found the long nightdress and laid it out ready as before, with her duffel.

'Two can play at that game,' she thought. 'And now . . . now what . . .?'

Tonight she would need some extra thing for her protection, as in a fairy tale or legend. World had talked of a key that she alone had. Now she knew that the winged boy, wrestling with time, was that key. But tonight she must hold some other secret object, a talisman, something that would keep her safe when the final moves in the game were set in motion. She had a sense of a great black and silver wind that would rush through the garden, of statues giving voice, the world translated.

She closed her eyes and waited for inspiration. When none came, she opened them, and scanned about the room for clues. Still she was blank. She gritted her teeth.

'Come on, come *on*!'

The shadows were already lengthening, the tryst by the moondial was only hours away.

In the end, unable to contain her restlessness, she went downstairs where Aunt Mary sat comfortably stitching.

'Where's the Raven? Miss Raven, I mean.'

'Oh, just popped over to the House. She said she wanted to hand something in to the Lost Property.'

'Oh. What?'

'A watch, she said. Found it in the graveyard.'

Minty saw in her mind's eye Tom removing the telltale watch from his thin wrist, pushing it into his pocket. She saw the threadbare cuffs of the jacket, the ragged holes. And she saw again the long orange flight of the cat.

Tom, alone now in that stone maze under the ground as the shadows thickened ... Tom, putting his hand into his pocket for the comforting feel of the watch that alone could show him the time. Perhaps he had already discovered his loss.

'Oh, poor Tom!'

She must have said the words out loud.

'Why, Minty, you're crying,' she heard Aunt Mary say. 'What is it, dear?'

Minty felt the tears slide silently down.

'Nothing.' She stared hopelessly at the kind, inquiring face, sensing the gulf between them, the unsayable words. 'I'll just go out for a bit, I think.'

She went almost mechanically to the churchyard, her thoughts in turmoil. She made a list of reasons why she should not visit the moondial that night. The Raven would be abroad, stalking near-invisible in her black cloak. Tom no longer had the watch she had given him. He might not be there. Then, last but most powerful, a strong fear, that she herself might be lost forever, might be drawn irrevocably out of time.

Then came a crowd of memories. Tom, grinning one moment, racked with coughing the next. Tom, nearly blue with cold in the snow, but desperate to reach her. Then that small hooded figure, singing in the moonlight, kneeling over the long pool, cowering in that bare yellow room.

She remembered too Kate's faint smile, half-open eyes, and that was when she made up her mind. That morning she had been given her heart's desire. Now she would help Tom and Sarah to reach theirs.

'Lots of things are stronger than fear – love for a start.'

This was the test. Love against fear, and against time itelf.

Feeling a sudden chill, the prickling of her arms into gooseflesh, she realized that she was by the church tower, and instinctively she lifted her eyes. The gilt pennants stood motionless, reflecting the low sun. And as she stood looking at them an answer came into her mind unbidden.

'Yes!' she whispered. 'That's it!'

She knew now what she must take with her on that most dangerous journey. She had the talisman.

She placed it carefully in the pocket of her duffel. Now she was ready armed against whatever dark powers she might encounter. There was no doubt in her mind that she was going into battle. She had glimpsed the forces of evil in that mocking, hooded throng, in the glittering eyes of Miss Vole. Now she was to meet them head on.

As before, she lay and feigned sleep when Aunt Mary made her nightly round. Miss Raven, she knew, intended to leave the house some time after this. Minty was counting on her, too, wanting to be in Belton by midnight. She was somewhere downstairs, waiting. Only when she had gone could Minty herself make her move.

She watched the clock, strained her ears for any sound of movement. Quarter to eleven. Then the church clock struck the hour. Five past. Ten past. She stood by the window and saw the moon hanging high above the trees, and could smell the dank green odours of the night rising powerfully from the garden. Once a car passed, the beam of its headlights eerily illuminating the hedges and verges.

Now the luminous digits on her clock showed eleven twenty-seven. On the church clock the fingers would be spreading to form that almost straight line which was to have been Tom's signal to set out. She imagined him waiting in a different time and another dark, and prayed that he would come.

The half hour struck. This was when Minty had counted on leaving. If she ran, she could reach the moondial in ten minutes, perhaps even less. She wondered how late she dared leave it. Her heart began to pound at the thought that she might have to steal from her room and down the stairs, past Miss Raven, with the possibility of discovery at every step.

'But it's what I'll do, if I have to,' she told herself. 'Even if she sees me. I'll just rush straight out of the door and run and run! She'd never catch me!'

Certainly not by any human means.

Then came a soft click. Minty stiffened. A band of yellow light fell across the path almost directly under her window. Another click. Minty shrank back behind the curtains.

A tall black shape glided swiftly down the path. At the gate it turned, and she glimpsed the pallid face, looking back towards the sleeping house.

After a time, evidently satisfied, the figure slipped through the gate and made towards the main drive to the House. Minty let out a long-held breath.

'At least she's gone that way!'

She went softly from her room and down the stairs to the hall, where a light still burned. In the sitting room she eased open the low casement window she had earmarked earlier. A moment later and she stood on the soft earth under the sill, half dizzied by the overpowering scent of roses.

At the gate she glanced briefly to the right. The street was empty, marvellously hushed and innocent, as she turned her steps towards the church.

There, as she had expected, she found the cats again. They stalked between the yews or lay motionless on tombs, basking in the moonlight. Here and there she glimpsed a silvered eye. The cats did not turn a hair at her presence. Each was locked in a private world, intent on his own secret.

Already she felt the hem of her nightdress wet and cold as it swished through the long grass. She stumbled on over stone and hummock, her eyes

straining ahead for the shattered stone window. She had no thought and no fears, only the urgent need to go on, to reach the moondial.

Once she had scrambled through the now-familiar opening she paused for an instant. She saw that the distances of the park were bathed in a curiously soft, milky light. The horizons were misty and insubstantial as a dream. But her legs went forward as if of their own accord and as she drew near the moondial she saw, standing by it, a solitary dark figure. For a moment her heart stopped.

'No! Oh no!'

Her legs were still carrying her onwards and then she saw that it was not the Raven but – incredibly and miraculously – Tom! He was waiting for her, had kept his promise, no matter how. And as she went to meet him she thought that this was the first time she had ever discovered him, a waiting figure in a landscape. Before, he had always come and gone in the twinkling of an eye.

And so for the first time she actually went to meet

him. He evidently had not seen her, and when she softly called his name he turned suddenly and she saw his face brighten, the half-fearful joy.

'Oh Tom!'

'Minty!'

Half-sobbing, half-laughing, they clung to one another.

'Tom! You came! The watch!' She could feel him shivering, and knew that she, too, was trembling.

'Lost it, didn't I?'

'I know, and I thought—'

'But I ain't daft!' He stood back then and regarded her with the old triumphant look. 'S'easy! Fingers in a line on an arm clock – fingers in a line on a *house* clock!'

She laughed with him, in sheer relief.

'You came, an' all!'

'You – didn't you know I would?'

He shrugged.

'Never tell. Not wiv a girl.'

'Oh –*you*!'

He was clapping his arms across his chest now to

stop his shivering, and darting uneasy looks about the quiet garden.

'Now what?' he asked.

'I – don't know.'

Her eyes travelled beyond him to where the moondial lay newly sculpted by moonlight. He followed her gaze.

'That.'

'Yes.'

Slowly they both approached. They stood regarding the winged man and the boy.

'It's the little 'un, you said ...' Tom sounded dubious.

'Yes. I know who he is now.'

'Bit cissy ... all them curls! *He'll* never be a footman!'

'No.'

She looked at Tom, his face wary again, half-suspicious.

'But it's him that'll help us. Come on.'

She stretched out her own hand and laid it on the moonbleached head. She thought, 'For the last time!'

Tom was watching her, still uncertain.

'Come on. Now you!'

Ever so slowly, as if expecting to be burned, he put out his own hand and laid it next to hers. Minty silently said the words she had read in the book World had given her and had memorized, as a charm:

'Light and shadow by turns, but always love.'

Next moment she was reeling in a long green corridor of time. Her ears filled with the old whispers and voices, and that strong wind blew clean and cold. She was drinking it in and it tasted white in her mouth. She was swimming in it like a fish.

When the wind dropped and the voices faded Minty knew that they were in a different season, and under a different moon. The air was sharp, frosty, and strong with the reek of autumn. The moon shone full over trees half-leaved, littered lawns and paths.

'S'cold!' she heard Tom whisper. Then a sharp tug at her sleeve. 'Look!'

She followed his pointing finger and saw, moving slowly along the terrace, a small cloaked figure.

'Sarah!'

It had worked! All three of them were brought together, the stage was set. Minty felt in her pocket for her talisman.

Tonight Sarah did not sing. The pair watched as she turned and descended the steps into the garden.

''Ere! Where's she going?'

Sarah, instead of taking the usual path, had stepped behind one of the dark yews. For an instant she disappeared from view. Then she reappeared, moving diagonally away from them, over the lawns.

'The orangery!' whispered Minty, but even as she spoke could not believe that Sarah was making for that place of reflecting glass.

'After her!' whispered Tom.

They followed, keeping their distance, slipping from shadow to shadow.

'Poor Mary sits a-weeping, a-weeping,
*   a-weeping,*
Poor Mary sits a-weeping on a bright
*   summer's day.'*

The song drifted over the quiet acres.

'Oh what is she a-weeping for, a-weeping
*   for, a-weeping for,*
Oh what is she a-weeping for, on a bright
*   summer's day?'*

Now the small figure was in full moonlight.
'She's going to that pond!' whispered Tom.

'She's weeping for a playmate, a playmate,
*   a playmate,*
She's weeping for a playmate on this bright
*   summer's day!'*

As the song ended the figure stopped. There
before her, paces away, was the circular pool. And

now, Minty saw, it was filled with water. It lay perfectly calm, smooth as polished silver, smooth as a mirror.

'One more time I'll try,' they heard the child say. 'The magic night of all the year . . . Hallowe'en!'

At the word Minty felt a thrill of terror. They had come to Hallowe'en, when all the spirits in the world were let loose! The air seemed suddenly crowded with invisible presences. Again she felt for the reassurance of the talisman.

'Hallowe'en!' she heard Tom gasp. 'Lor-save us!'

He gripped her arm and she knew that he, who half-believed in the devil, was a thousand times more terrified than she.

Now Sarah advanced slowly to the edge of the pool and knelt. Lowering her head, she again began the ritual bathing of her face. The watchers saw her haloed by moonlit droplets, and willed the charm to work.

So intent were they that they did not notice the first strange shapes steal from the shadows where they had stood concealed. From all directions they came, silently assembling as if at a secret signal. They slid from behind tree and wall, from the watery depths of the orangery. They were forming a ring, closing in on that solitary little figure by the pool.

Sarah, all unaware, at last lifted her face, and tilted it up to the moon, as she had to the sun.

Now, at last, the two watchers saw that host of other shapes. They clutched at one another, frozen.

The figures, real or unreal, were those of children, and they were cloaked. They had no faces. Each wore a mask, grotesque and horrible, with cavernous sockets instead of eyes. Some had horns. Then, one by one, weird orange glows emerged from the folds of the cloaks. Round and luminous, disembodied heads.

Minty felt Tom tugging at her arm, dragging her away.

'No! We mustn't run!'

Now, pumpkin lanterns raised, the shapes began a slow step-stepping round the pool. The whispering began:

'Devil's child, devil's child, devil's child!'

Sarah, still rapt under the moon, seemed not to hear. Inexorably the ring was closing in. The water of the pool began to blaze as the orange light spilled into its depths.

Now the whispered chant had changed:

'The devil's coming, devil's coming, devil's coming!'

Sarah, kneeling in their midst, at last shook her head and came to. They saw her stare wildly about her, heard her scream.

Then she was up and running, straight through the ring, and Tom and Minty went with her. The circle broke up with screams and yells.

'After her!'

''Ware the evil eye!'

'Drown her! Drown her!'

Sarah, blinded by terror, ran straight up to the curved wall with the stone basins and the lion mask.

She stumbled against it head on as Tom and Minty reached her.

'No! Oh no!' She beat against it with her fists.

'Sarah! We're here!' Minty reached and took hold of her, but she struggled to free herself. Her eyes met Minty's and instinctively she wrenched away her hand and put it to her stained cheek.

Breathless they stood at bay, all three, while the masks advanced, lights bobbing. When they were a few paces off, they stopped. Minty could feel Sarah clinging to her, frantically burrowing into her. There was a silence.

Minty forced herself to look at those hideous masks, one by one, livid white and yellow, slashed with black, green and red. She sensed the pair of eyes looking out from behind each one. Now she must play her part.

'Do you know who I am?' Her voice was a whisper. 'We have met before! I am Araminta Cane, and I am a ghost!'

As she hissed the last word a stir went through the listeners.

'I'm frit! I'm off!'

A small figure broke ranks and fled, dropping his lantern as he fled. The pumpkin lay rocking, glowing on the stone.

'She ain't a ghost!'

'Who's that other one?'

'Get them!'

Excited whispers ran about the semi-circle.

'Do as I say,' Minty went on, 'and you will not be harmed!'

They waited, watchful and intent.

'Soon the clock will strike midnight – midnight on Hallowe'en!'

At this they seemed to cower, huddle closer together.

'Do as I say. Go back to the pool, and drop your lanterns in the water. Then, as the clock begins to strike, shut your eyes. If you open them before the last stroke, then—'

She paused.

'The *devil*'ll get you!' Tom at her side suddenly thrust forward his face and hissed.

They jumped, all of them, but still they hesitated. Minty took another breath. This was their last chance.

'Quickly!' she ordered. 'Before it's too late!'

'The devil's coming! The devil's coming!'

Now they broke up in panic, pushing, screaming, stumbling in their haste. Down to the pool they ran pellmell and one by one they threw their lanterns in. They hissed and darkened as they met the water. As the last one died, the hour began to strike.

Minty saw the children stop stockstill. They stood frozen in tableau, as if in a game of musical statues. She knew that their eyes were shut tight against the coming of the devil.

'Quick! Now!'

They had only the space of the twelve strokes of the hour to make their escape. Hand in hand they sped away, over the bare, silvered lawns towards the shelter of the trees, running to cover. As she went Minty counted the hour's strokes ... ten ... eleven ... twelve!

'Get down!'

They crouched, fighting for breath, within the low boughs of a spreading fir tree.

'Tricked!'

'They've gone!'

'They tricked us!'

'Find 'em!'

The search began. All about the hidden trio dark shapes darted, searching, lifting branches, peering. Through the screen of boughs Minty saw to her horror a masked face looming above, only feet away. She ducked, hiding the telltale pallor of her face. Head buried, she felt the thundering of her own heart. She caught a muttered 'Pesky devils!' then, after a moment, a cry, 'Hey, Sam!'

She braced herself, ready to run again.

'Sam! I'm off out of this!'

Another voice, 'Me, 'n all! Reckon – d'you reckon the devil *has* got 'em? What if he gets us!'

There was a yelp.

'Come on – scarper!'

There was the thunder of retreating feet on turf and yells from all directions.

'Beat it!'

'Run!'

'Devil's after us!'

The voices faded, one by one they dissolved. Minty eased her cramped limbs and watched the other two cautiously unbury themselves.

'They've gone!' Tom sat back suddenly. 'Phew!'

Sarah sat perfectly still, her hood pulled over her head and face. Minty crawled from under the branches and stood. She stooped and held out a hand.

'Come on, Sarah. They've gone.'

After a hesitation Sarah put out her hand and Minty pulled her to her feet. Tom scrambled out after them.

Still holding Sarah's hand, Minty began to walk towards the moondial and journey's end. She could see it ahead, felt it pulling her like a magnet. When they reached it they stopped and stood, all three of them uncertain of the next move.

'Sarah!' said Minty softly. 'You can put your hood down now.'

'Safe as houses!' said Tom encouragingly, he who had never known a safe house in his life. 'Honest!'

'I ... I daren't ...' came a muffled voice from the hood. 'Don't want to harm you. You're – my friends.'

Over the hood Tom's eyes met Minty's.

'Yes,' said Minty. 'Please, Sarah. Please.'

A long pause. Then slowly, very slowly, a hand came up and pulled the hood away. Sarah, her stained face clear in the moonlight, looked wonderingly first at one, then at the other.

Then, quite deliberately, Minty leaned towards her and kissed her, full on the marked cheek.

She withdrew. Sarah was staring up at her in disbelief. Now, at last, Minty put her hand in her pocket and drew out her talisman. It shone broadly, catching the moonlight.

Sarah gasped, her hands flew up to cover her eyes.

''Ware the glass! A mirror!'

'Sarah. Sarah. Open your eyes.'

Minty's eyes met those of Tom.

'Sarah!' he coaxed in turn. 'Look – come all this long way I have, to fetch you! I – I want you to be my sweetheart! Will you?'

There was no sign, but a tear glinted beneath the tightly pressed fingers.

Minty tried again.

'Sarah! You must trust us! Please!'

A long silence. Then, with a shuddering sob, Sarah let her hands fall. She looked into Minty's face.

'I'm holding the mirror.' Minty heard her voice tremble. 'I want you to look into it. Don't be afraid.'

'Here!' Tom grabbed Sarah's hand and held it.

'Trust me, Sarah. You must!'

Then at last, her face full of dread, Sarah turned her eyes from Minty's and looked full into the mirror. She gazed and gazed as if she would never stop. Then her free hand went up and touched the glass, very gently.

'That's – me?'

'That's you, Sarah.'

The hand moved from mirror to face, then

back again. She fingered her hair, pale as corn, and touched her eyes, lips, cheek. She was alone with herself for the first time in her life, the others forgotten.

'I'm – beautiful!'

'Oh you are, you are!' Minty half-sobbed.

'And – the mirror – it didn't crack!'

'Course it didn't!' Tom was alight, triumphant, as if he himself had worked the miracle.

As they stood looking one to another, a voice rang out.

'Sarah! Sarah!'

They whirled about, all three. There, advancing swiftly along the terrace, was that tall black figure of a woman.

'Oh!' Instinctively Sarah's hands flew back to her face. She started towards the House. But Tom and Minty pulled her back, held her firm.

'No!'

'Not this time!' said Tom fiercely.

The terrible figure was descending the steps now, advancing swiftly up the path between the yews.

'Oh, I must go!' sobbed Sarah.

'No! Come with me! Sarah!' Tom pulled her right out of Minty's grasp. Then he too bent and kissed her. 'Come along with me! Won't you?'

Minty stood alone to face the advancing woman, cloak swirling about her.

'Sarah! Here, this instant! Devil's child that you are!'

Tom and Sarah clung together. The woman was almost upon them now, her face making itself into features, mouth, nose, eyes.

Minty stepped forward, shielding the others. Just as the woman reached them, that wild white face barely inches away, Minty lifted the mirror and held it full in her path.

''Ware the devil!' she cried. ''Ware the evil eye!'

There was a scream, the sharp splintering of glass, and then followed an enormous hush, as if for a moment the world had stopped turning.

Afterwards Minty remembered only dimly what happened, as if it had been a dream. She remembered a shrivelled black heap on the ground where the woman had stood, and a great black and silver wind rushing through the garden, stirring it into life. The very stone of the statues seemed to turn to flesh, to ease and breathe. At the far end of the walk a dove was released into the air.

Incredulously she followed its flight as it soared skyward, then, hearing her name called, saw Tom and Sarah, hand in hand, running away and already in a mist. They turned their heads and smiled and waved. For an instant she was jealous, tempted to go after them, run free forever in moontime, always a child, in a world without change.

Then her eye fell on the moondial and she felt its pull, powerfully drawing her back. She stood torn. And as she stood she thought afterwards that she remembered another child running out of the milky mists, a tiny figure, calling:

'Teddy! Teddy!'

Then Tom's shout of joy.

'Dorrie! It's our Dorrie!'

Then the three figures meeting and embracing and running on again, on and on and out of sight.

Minty did not remember touching the winged boy, nor even the last long green turning of time, the winds and the lost voices. She was by the moondial, and alone. The silence was absolute. She felt tears cold on her cheek.

'It's done!' she said out loud.

The strange game was over. The last moves had been played. She must make her own way back in the moonlight, alone. She turned her face towards the churchyard and on impulse lightly touched the silvery stone curls of the winged boy.

'We won!' she told him, and began the journey home. She had been to Hallowe'en and back, and was tired.

EPILOGUE

Next morning Minty found in the pocket of her duffel the mirror she had taken with her as talisman. It was splintered. When she went downstairs, breakfast was already over and Miss Raven had gone. Aunt Mary seemed not at all surprised. Minty was even less so.

'She didn't vanish into thin air, did she?' she asked.

'Of course not, dear. She took Mr Jones's taxi to the station.'

'She didn't have a big ginger cat on her shoulder?'

'Oh Minty!' her aunt sighed. 'The things you say!'

Nevertheless she smiled.

'I must say you look quite different this morning,' she said. 'It must have been that nice long sleep. You look quite – washed clean. That's what my mother used to say.'

Minty smiled. She knew that she had woken from quite another sleep, from a long enchantment.

The telephone rang, and Aunt Mary went to answer it. As she waited, Minty thought how long ago, what centuries ago, that other call seemed, the one that had started it all.

'It's the hospital! It's your mother – oh Minty, she's asking for you!'

The circle was almost complete. At the very moment when Tom and Sarah had been set free, to run forever in moontime, Kate, too, had been released from her spell.

'Mr Benson will be here in an hour, to take you to her.'

'I'll go out, till then,' Minty told her. 'I've got one or two things to do.'

She went first to the lodge, where World was setting up his chair and table, ready for the day ahead. She watched his slow, patient movements, pictured his face when she told him. But as he looked up she saw that he already knew.

'Well, then,' he said. 'I was right. You did have the key.'

'Yes. It's done. They're free.'

'Well done, then,' he said.

'And my mother – she's awake – she's asking for me!'

He laughed.

'And why wouldn't she be? Oh, I'm glad, I am glad. So the work's done.'

'Yes.' They seemed always to talk in a kind of shorthand, but each knowing exactly what the other meant. 'I'm just going to the garden again.'

'Tie up loose ends?' he suggested.

'Yes.'

She walked on.

'You bring that mother of yours here to see me, when she's on her feet again!' he called after her. 'I've got a thing or two to tell her about you!'

She turned her head.

'But I expect she already knows she's got a good 'un!'

When Minty entered the garden she half-knew

what to expect. On her first visit she had been instantly aware that it was waiting for her, expectant, thronging with secrets. Now it lay perfectly calm and rinsed. It was no longer calling to her.

She walked slowly along the broad terrace and when she reached the seven shallow steps she lifted her eyes and saw that the stone dove that had been released to fly through the dark air only hours before was again frozen in motion on that uplifted arm. She raised her own arm to it in salute as she descended.

Halfway down the path she stopped, looked to left and right. She had almost expected to find that they had gone, that she had only imagined those cruel masks with their slitted eyes. Now, in the sunlight, they held no terror, but they were still there, inexplicable among the harmless fruit and flowers. Again she looked at them, first to left, then to right.

'Miss Raven ...?' she wondered. 'And Miss Vole ...?'

Then to the moondial itself, whose power had worked miracles. It gave no sign of the struggle that had so recently taken place at its very foot. Those two impassive winged figures stood locked in their struggle as though they would stand through eternity. Minty stood and gazed at them, as if for the last time. They held a message, and now she understood it. She touched the cold head of the boy, though she expected no response, because there was no need.

'It was Hallowe'en last night!' she told him, and moved away under the strong July sun.

Then on to the churchyard, where it had all begun. She went to the corner by the tower and found that the tiny icy tongues were still there, as she had known they would be. For what seemed like the thousandth time she tilted back her head to see those gilt pennants, stockstill in a windless air.

'It's a mystery!' she said out loud.

There was one last leap to be made in the dark. The first mystery was the last. She wheeled about, sensing that the answer was a fingertip away.

Her eye fell again on that tiny, thumbnail headstone, with its stark inscription: E. L. 1871.

Only a child, she thought, could be marked by such a stone, an unloved child, with so bleak a memorial. Then, as she gazed, there came a picture of Tom, dancing in the long grass, yelling, 'And pigs can fly and the moon's made of green cheese and I'll be six foot high yet or my name ain't Teddy Larkin!'

He seemed so real, so near, that she could have put out a hand and touched him.

'Of course! Teddy. Edward – Edward Larkin!

And mingled with the realization another memory, of that day when he had suddenly appeared here, on this very corner and shivered and said, 'As if someone was walking on my grave!'

Then the memory of Tom and Sarah, hand in hand, running off through the mists into moontime, to meet Dorrie.

Full circle.

If you enjoyed

Moondial,

why not read more
Faber Children's
Classics . . .

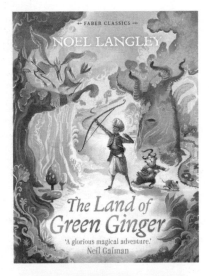

FABER CLASSICS

NOEL LANGLEY

The Land of
Green Ginger

'A glorious magical adventure.'
Neil Gaiman

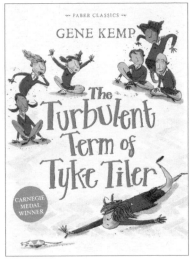

FABER CLASSICS

GENE KEMP

The
Turbulent
Term of
Tyke Tiler

CARNEGIE
MEDAL
WINNER

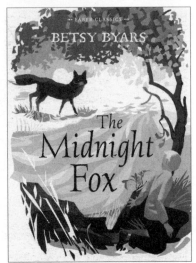

FABER CLASSICS

BETSY BYARS

The
Midnight
Fox

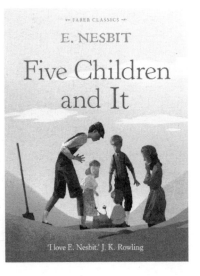

FABER CLASSICS

E. NESBIT

Five Children
and It

'I love E. Nesbit.' J. K. Rowling